To Mark, Maddie, and Jethro for

CINDY DORMINY

In a Nutshell

In a Nutshell

Red Adept Publishing, LLC

104 Bugenfield Court

Garner, NC 27529

https://RedAdeptPublishing.com/

Copyright © 2021 by Cindy Dorminy. All rights reserved.

COVER ART BY Streetlight Graphics[1]

No part of this book may be reproduced, scanned, or distributed in any printed or electronic form without permission. Please do not participate in or encourage piracy of copyrighted materials in violation of the author's rights. Thank you for respecting the hard work of this author.

This is a work of fiction. Names, characters, places, and incidents either are the product of the author's imagination or are used fictitiously, and any resemblance to locales, events, business establishments, or actual persons—living or dead—is entirely coincidental.

---

1. http://StreetlightGraphics.com

CHAPTER ONE

Mitch

Nothing says "I'm not interested" more clearly than moving to Africa. During the two months, one week, and four days since she left without a backward glance, I worked my way through the stages of grief, hanging out in the depression phase far too long, and eventually made it to the fifth and final stage. Reading Gunnar's email from his cousin today slams me back into the anger category faster than a buttered bullet. It's not like we had a thing going, but I really thought we made some headway. My romance-o-meter is definitely broken.

The lake is usually my happy place, but it's not cutting it today. Even though it's still warm on an early fall day, my body feels cold and dead inside, so much that not even a glorious sunset with pinks and oranges streaking across the sky and reflecting off the lake water can calm my soul.

I shove the phone back into Gunnar's hands as I scoff. "She says, 'Tell Mitch I'm sorry.' That's it?"

He sits beside me as we watch the water from the lake lap near our feet while a boat buzzes past. His bare feet make indentations in the wet sand. "Sorry, bro. It sucks."

Clenching my jaws to keep from spewing words about Melanie that I *wouldn't* be sorry for, I pick up a stick and toss it down the beach so Griff, the local dog, will play fetch. That shaggy mutt never lets me down. He's always around when I need to bend someone's ear. I thought Dr. Mel Ballard's attitude toward me was starting to thaw, but it wasn't enough to move me out of the friend zone by a long shot.

After a long stretch of silence and a hefty sigh, I say, "I know I've asked you before, but, Gunnar, did she—"

"Nope. We were all blindsided. My cousin is gone, and she's not coming back." He scoffs. "Even her father was shocked into silence."

"Oh, to have been a fly on the wall when he found out..."

"No kidding. I think this is the first time my cousin has ever done anything without the elder Dr. Ballard's blessing."

Griff trudges toward me, dragging a stick almost as big as he is, and I reward him with a belly rub. "If she wanted to get away from me, she could have just moved to Jacksonville, not gone to Somalia."

Gunnar chuckles while he scratches underneath Griff's chin. "That would be still within her father's reach."

I roll my eyes at the lame excuse.

"Besides, Doctors Without Borders is huge. Think of all the good she'll do."

Leave it to Gunnar to throw a positive spin on the situation. "I know."

"Enough about her. What's done is done, and your real friends are still here."

Truer words were never spoken. Smithville would be just another dinky town on the map if it weren't for the awesome people who cared for me and my brothers when our world fell apart around us at an early age.

"Hey," Andie yells, snapping me out of my thoughts. She saunters from their massive log home to where we're sitting along the shore. "I was wondering where you went."

Andie, the newest member of Smithville, moved here to take over her grandmother's shop, and won Gunnar's heart in the process. The entire town adores her, including myself, and it's nice to have a human to talk over my problems, someone who hasn't known me since I was just a twinkle in my sorry excuse for a father's eye.

Andie plops down in Gunnar's lap and gives him a big, sloppy kiss with a massive "mwah." They are still in the lovey-dovey phase of their engagement, and while I'm happy for both of them, it's more than I can handle today. I wish Gunnar would take out his service revolver and shoot me in the foot. *Not. In. The. Mood.*

I squeeze my eyes closed. "Guys, I'm right here."

Andie leans over and gives me a side hug. "I'm sorry. I just get the 'can't help its' when I'm around my big ole teddy bear."

Gunnar shows Andie the email, and with her eyebrows pulled together, she reads the message from Mel. "I'm sorry, Mitch. I had no idea. She seemed happy, but I guess it shows we never know what's going on inside someone else's head. I do believe something good will come out of this."

"Harrumph."

Andie throws the stick, and Griff takes off in search of it. "What did she mean by 'I'm sorry'?"

"I have no idea."

"No telling." Gunnar snuggles with Andie.

"Sorry for leading me on? Sorry for not saying goodbye?"

Gunnar shrugs while he stares out over the lake at the setting sun. "I can't believe anyone would ever want to leave this place. It's serene, and the community is like one big family. There's nothing I don't like about Smithville, even if the opportunities are scarce."

Andie nudges my shoulder with hers. "I think you need a woman."

I hold out my hands to stop her train of thought. "Oh no. That's the last thing I need. I've waited and hoped and crushed on one girl for ten years, like a stupid third grader, and I'm not going down that road again."

"How about no strings attached?"

Andie gasps and smacks her fiancé on the shoulder. "That is *not* what he needs. It didn't do you any good, did it?"

Gunnar grimaces, and I imagine he's remembering his skirt-chasing days as he was trying to get over an ex. But that was before Andie rambled into town and turned his life upside down in the best possible ways. "Yeah, not my proudest moments—that's for sure. Focus on your job. You're the best EMT in Smithville."

"That is true." Andie stands and dusts the sand from her jeans. "What I think would help is if you had your own place. Silas's house is busting at the seams with two boys and a newborn, and Clint is obviously not using the apartment above my shop anymore. You're welcome to it."

My younger brother is definitely not spending any time in the second-story studio apartment above In a Jam. Every time his fiancée shows up for her shift at the hospital, it's obvious Regina isn't getting much sleep. I'm glad they reconnected, and I'm so lucky to have both my brothers living in the same town as me again, but like Andie said, living with my older brother, his wife, and his three kids is getting a bit cramped.

I mull over her offer. "I think I'll take you up on that offer. Thanks."

Her smile broadens like she's solved all of my problems. "Regina says you make the best buttermilk pie that is pretty much a must-have at the fall festival."

I groan. "Not this year. Just not in the mood."

Andie's mouth turns down in a pout. "Please. I heard it's to die for."

She is hard to resist with those puppy-dog eyes. "I don't know. It's not that special."

Gunnar leans over and stage-whispers, "It actually *is* that special."

"And I'll let you use the shop's kitchen to bake if you want to spread out."

If for no other reason than to pacify her, I say, "I'll think about it."

Looking satisfied with my answer, she grins. "Yes! I'll let you two burly dudes get back to your man talk."

Andie jogs away from us, and I catch Gunnar watching her every step. *He's a changed man.* He would move heaven and earth for Andie. It appears as though I'll be the perpetual bachelor of Smithville, though.

As if he can read my mind, Gunnar nudges me with his shoulder. "You have to let her go. Move on."

His words are true, but damn, they hurt, like a knife straight to the heart. I wasted so many years hoping something would happen, and now it's clear I need to get over it. So I force myself back into the acceptance phase, whether I like it or not.

Even if I don't completely believe my own words, I say, "You're right. I can't change what happened, so I have to keep moving forward." With an almost-genuine smile, I add, "Life has never been easy for me, but I won't let anything stop me, certainly not a woman."

Gunnar holds out his fist for me to knuckle bump. "That's the spirit." He pats me on the back as he stands to leave. "Nothing my cousin did changes us. You got that?"

"Thanks, bro."

Gunnar saunters toward his lakefront home while I stay on the beach, petting Griff, all alone in my thoughts. With a father who's a drug dealer locked up in the federal pen and a mother who left three children behind to chase a boyfriend across the country, seeing one dream fade away shouldn't feel so difficult to manage.

I give Griff one last rub under his chin then rise and head back to my truck. It's time to shake out of this funk, and the best medicine for that is to hold my baby niece. Nothing says love like cuddling a newborn baby.

CHAPTER TWO

Jackie

As I walk across the parking lot, my Kate Spade laptop bag slides off my shoulder, almost making me drop the drink carrier perched in one hand. The purple gift bag dangles from the bend in my elbow as I wedge my cell phone between my shoulder and ear.

"You have a good week, too, Dad. See you soon."

I slip through the door of the Southeastern Hospital Association and scurry to catch the elevator before it shuts on me. While I wait for the doors to slide open on the twentieth floor, I stare at my reflection in the mirrored walls. Part of my unruly red hair has already escaped my bun. Matthew hates it when anyone is late for the Monday progress meeting, but I desperately need to do two things before I go to the boardroom: drop off my surprise to Penny and fix my crazy mop of hair.

"Hey there." Penny sits at her desk outside Matthew's office. She's so cute with her jet-black bob and flawless complexion. No matter how stressful my day is, I can always count on her smile to cheer me up.

I hold out the drink carrier. "Happy Monday."

She clutches her chest. "You're the sweetest." Penny takes a sip of her caramel macchiato, and her eyes roll back in her head. "Mmm, perfection."

"Oh, and I got you this." I hand her the gift bag. "While Mom and I were doing our weekly yard sale run, I saw this and couldn't pass it up."

Penny laughs. "I still can't believe Little Miss Ladder Climber scrounges through other people's stuff to save a buck."

8

No matter how big my bank account is, a bargain is a bargain, and I love to tell Penny about my weekly deals. A month ago, my mother found four Adderley teacups with matching saucers that were in mint condition. And the owner was only asking five dollars for all of them. I've never seen my mother whip out a Lincoln so fast, but when she has a chance to add to her collection, she becomes like a kid in a candy store.

"I thought you could use it with your..." I peer around the corner to make sure no one is within earshot. I whisper, "With your Kaori costume."

When Penny pulls out the quarter violin, her jaw drops and her lip trembles. "It's so cute, but I can't accept this."

Readjusting my bun, I say, "Yes, you can. There was no way I could walk away from it." I point to the crack on the back. "This is probably why I got it for a steal."

She waves me off. "Who cares? This is so—"

"Taking violin lessons?" Brett, a colleague of mine, asks. He's the biggest pain in my backside, but since I've known him longer than I care to admit, I put up with his peskiness. Besides, he's all bark and no bite.

Penny chews her lip. If he ever found out she cosplays, he would never let her live it down. I think it's great she lets loose and does something people wouldn't normally expect from her. Maybe if he did that, he might be able to keep a girlfriend for more than a week. Maybe I should let my hair down more often, as well.

"I found it for her nephew. He's five, and this is a good starter instrument."

Brett shivers. "I hope his parents have good earplugs."

As he walks toward the boardroom, Penny and I knuckle-bump.

"Got to get ready for the meeting. See you in there." I wave over my shoulder as I hustle to my office to prepare for the day.

IF BRETT CLICKS HIS pen one more time during this meeting, I'll go nuclear on him. His arrogant smirk makes me sense he knows something the rest of us in the meeting don't. For reasons I don't understand, other than the good-ole-boy network, he has been promoted twice in the last two years. I've been at Southeast Hospital Association for three years longer than he has, and I'm still waiting on my jump to VP. In fact, if it weren't for my recommendation, he would still be with the worst ambulance-chaser firm in Atlanta.

As Matthew McGuire, our boss, enters the room, Brett speeds up his clicking, and I snatch the pen out of his hand. His mouth drops like I just stole his ice cream. He'll get over it.

Matthew clears his throat as Penny, his assistant, who has the patience of Job, passes out our quarterly report documents. Matthew bangs on his keyboard with his sausage fingers then shoves his laptop toward her. "Penny, have you messed this machine up again?"

"No sir," she replies as she rushes to his aid. Her hands tremble as she types on the keyboard. As usual, she's able to unlock the laptop and open the presentation.

I feel sorry for her, and since we're the only beings in the room with ovaries, we have to stick together. Our eyes meet, and I give her a pathetic smile of solidarity.

"Okay, folks. I'll just cut to the chase. As you already know, hospitals across the region are having to tighten their belts."

God, I hate his buzzwords. I should start a Bingo card with all the phrases he uses. Not a meeting goes by without him using at least one "touch base," "best practices," or my favorite, "paradigm shift." I cringe even thinking those words.

"Our stockholders want us to make some tough decisions. Any ideas on how to make them happy?"

Brett raises his hand like he did when he was an eager fifth grader. "I have a great idea."

Everyone in the room turns to listen to him as he brownnoses. If there ever was a real-life Eddie Haskell, Brett is it. Always has been.

I roll my eyes, and Penny, who is sitting in the corner and taking notes, grins. I didn't know I was that obvious.

Brett sits taller, snatches his pen back from me, and clears his throat. "Stop taking Medicaid and Medicare patients."

Everyone in the group snickers.

"I'm serious. The administrative costs with those pesky programs are too high, and they can be easily be eliminated. Problem solved."

A few in the room have the gall to nod.

I sit tall in my chair. "There are better, more effective ways to trim the fat."

Now I'm using Matthew's catchphrases. His eyes bore into my soul, and this may be my chance to impress the boss. "What I'm saying is that there may be some overlap of services. We could look at hospitals that are close to one another that have the same specialized services. No need to duplicate efforts."

The room goes deathly quiet, and all eyes are on me, so I continue. "Perhaps, one hospital could focus on pediatrics, obstetrics, and so on, while another one focuses on ortho, oncology, cardiac."

Matthew grins. "I like it."

That corner office is going to be mine.

Never one to let me get the upper hand, Brett clicks his pen again and adds, "I'll go one step further. Why do we have two hospitals so close together? Just shut down an under-performing hospital altogether and funnel patients to the other facility. Same revenue, half the cost and we could even sell the property. Stockholders should love that."

Hushed tones around the room make me all jittery inside. Brett has some nerve, stealing my thunder and making it his own. When I cut my eyes toward Brett, he has the gall to wink. *Ugh.*

Matthew taps on his laptop until he reveals a map of all our SHA hospitals. He squints at the screen then points to several on the map. "These are within one hundred miles of one another. Penny, what's the population of Albany, Georgia?"

Penny's thumbs move across her phone with lightning speed. "A little over seventy-three thousand."

"And Tifton?"

She says, "Sixteen thousand seven hundred."

Brett snorts. "They're doomed."

"And what about Smithville?" Matthew asks.

Chewing on her lip, she searches on her phone. "A little less than eight thousand."

That's tiny.

Matthew pulls up the stats on Smithville Regional Hospital, and on paper, it doesn't look good.

"None of them are trauma centers," Bill Foster says as he studies the numbers. "I don't think it would be a huge loss for any of those towns."

Brett raises his hand again. Cue eye roll... again. "Sir, I would love to do an audit of the Albany site. My unique skill set will come in handy at this time. Bill's wife is about to have a baby any day now, and well, Tucker, you're just too green to handle making difficult decisions."

He's going to steamroll his way into getting promoted, and Matthew will sit back and let it happen because they're pals, golf buddies.

I raise my hand. *Can't believe I raised my hand.*

"Yes, Jackie?" Matthew asks.

"Sir, I think I should be the one to take charge of this project. I've worked hard, and I know the stats of that region better than anyone."

Matthew's gaze goes from me to Brett and back to me. After a long and painful moment of silence, he says, "Brett, you audit the Tifton site."

My jaw hits the floor. Brett gets everything he wants, just like when he was the teacher's pet in high school and wormed his way out of every group project. I can't stand people who take the easy way out and get rewarded for it.

Brett grins at me as if to say, "Works every time."

"Oh, and, Jackie," Matthew says, "I'm sending you to Smithville."

Yes! That's the no-brainer site.

"While we are at it, I think it's a good time to fill Dennis Paul's open slot after he retired last month. The person with the most convincing argument about their site will be promoted to VP."

Brett pumps his hand in the air like he's already won.

"I want you two to go about your mission a little differently than standard procedures." He taps a finger to his chin. "Instead of going in announced, giving the people time to prepare, I want it to be under the guise of writing an article for the *Atlanta Journal* or something stupid like that. Small-town people love to be noticed. Once you gain the trust of a few staff members, along with reviewing the data we already have, you should have a comprehensive analysis to present."

Nothing is going to get in my way. I've earned this promotion, and now I get a chance to prove what I'm made of, so I start my mental checklist on what I need to pack for Gooberville, USA. What's worse than a small town are the simple people who live there. Being chummy with the locals sounds like as much fun as getting a root canal, but if it gets me the VP position, I'll do it.

"I've got this in the bag," Brett mumbles to me.

Not one to shy away from a challenge, I say, "Brett, you need to get laid."

He snorts as he looks down his nose at us, but I'm not going to let him beat me out of the promotion of a lifetime. Nothing is going to get in my way this time. I've earned this, and I finally get a chance to prove I'm the most qualified person for the job.

CHAPTER THREE

Jackie

Driving down Interstate 75, I finish the third call from my father. He cannot stop telling me how proud of me he is for landing this project. If I get the promotion, I don't think we'll ever hear the end of it at our Sunday dinners. Being a judge, he always pushed me and my sister, Gretta, to reach for the stars, but I think she feels like she let him down by taking a leave of absence from her career to be a stay-at-home mom. "Can't do both well," she would tell me. She loves her children, but I get the feeling she's a little envious of my career advancements.

Always efficient, Penny answers her phone on the first ring. "Have you arrived there yet?"

I slam on my brakes for the tenth time since leaving Atlanta and honk my horn at the dude in the semi-truck who cut me off. He responds by tooting his horn back. "No, it's been traffic hell with one traffic jam after another. One time, it was a truck sitting on the side of the road with his load of siding sprawled out all over the interstate. At this rate, I'll make it to Smithville by the time I retire."

"Welcome to the world of commuting to work. You're lucky you've lived your entire life downtown." Her words are dipped in a tinge of jealousy.

"I don't know how people do this every day. My ulcer would be eating its way up my esophagus if I had to endure this on a regular basis."

Screeching to a halt again, my Mini Cooper misses the bumper of a beat-up truck by mere inches. "Can you check the highway traffic map to see what the hold-up is?"

"Pulling it up right now. Just so you know, Brett is already settled in his hotel in Tifton, ready to pounce on Monday."

"Overachiever." I should have been assigned to that site. Tifton is right off the interstate, making it easy for Brett to arrive, where the closest exit to Smithville is at least an extra hour and a half away. I'll have to poke through one small town after another at thirty miles an hour for the last leg of my trip.

Jerking my chin higher, I say, "He'll need the extra rest."

"Looks like you're about to pass another accident on the left side of the road. After that, it should be smooth sailing."

"Excellent. Thanks, Penny," I say as I merge in front of a sedan. I wave at the driver for letting me over. "I wish you could have come down here with me. I could use your guidance. Aren't you from somewhere down here?"

"Dothan, Alabama, and that is not anywhere near Smithville."

I let out a whimper. "But you understand small-town people better than me. I like the city, with grumpy jerks and smog and... Well, it's better than I make it sound."

"No, your assessment pretty much sums it up. I'd love to be there to soak up some Southern cooking. You're in for a treat."

"I'm there to work, so I doubt I'll have any time to do anything else."

She laughs. "Take time to enjoy the scenery, and I don't mean the trees."

Finally, I'm past the wreck and back to speed limit speed. "Not sure what you mean."

"Trust me. They grow 'em mighty fine down there. Mighty. Fine."

Imagining a nice butt in worn-out jeans and a nice twangy accent makes me a little flushed, and I'm glad Penny isn't here to witness it. "That may be true, but I'm here on business. Plus, men are usually intimidated by me."

She scoffs. "Whatever. Where you're staying is right on the main drag of town. It's called the Peach Fuzz Inn. It's only a few blocks from the hospital, so you will probably be able to park your car and walk to wherever you need to go."

"Sounds peachy, ha-ha. Get it?"

"You had two choices. That or the Elks Lodge."

"Fuzz it is. Can't wait." *If it gets me one step closer to my promotion, I'll stay in a barn.*

"Got to go. Boss man is yelling at me again."

Penny hangs up, cutting my last contact with the city as I'm finally able to exit the interstate to meander down the streets of one small town after another. At first, they're quaint with their Georgian columns, but they quickly switch to mid-century modern, then massive fields with one farmhouse every few miles.

After an hour of driving, with an empty tank and a full bladder, I pull up to a gas pump behind a large truck that has seen better days. The bumper is rusty, and one of the fenders is a different color than the rest of the truck. The owner wears ratty jeans and a denim shirt unbuttoned, exposing a tank undershirt spreading tight across his muscular chest. With a baseball cap worn backward, he leans against his truck, thumbs flying across his phone screen as he waits for his truck to fill up with gas. He groans, slides the phone into his back pocket, and rubs his temples.

While I go about filling up my tank, I feel his eyes on me. Mocking him, I lean against my car, cross my arms, and wait to catch him glancing my way. When he does, I politely say, "Hello."

He grunts.

"Nice day."

"If you say so."

I eye the sticker in the window of his truck: *Cute enough to stop your heart. Skilled enough to revive it.* I point to it. "Is that true? I mean, the first part definitely is, but... never mind."

My ears burn as red as my hair, and I scratch my neck as he lets out a chuckle. I focus on the gas meter, and my small tank fills up faster than his gas guzzler, so when I finish the transaction, I peek over to see him shaking his head.

"Is there something funny?"

He clears his throat then shrugs. "I've just never seen a car that small before. Did you pick it before it was ripe?"

My eyes grow wide as I process his words. His voice, as smooth as chocolate on a summer's day, sends a sensation through my body—one I don't need right now. I wave toward his monster truck and reply, "As opposed to yours that runs through fossil fuels so fast, I bet you get ten gallons to the mile."

His mouth twitches as he completes his transaction. "A person's choice of car says a lot about their character. You..." He waves a hand in my direction. "High maintenance."

I walk up to his truck and run a hand over the edge of the bed. "You might be right about that. That bumper sticker has cocky written all over it."

He holds his hands out in front of him in a defensive motion. "Hey there, missy. My sister-in-law gave that to me as a dirty Santa gift. I would hurt her feelings if I didn't use it."

Cocky, yet considerate. That's an interesting combination. I pat the tailgate and say, "Perhaps, but this vehicle tells me you're over-compensating for something." I scan down his solid body to add punch to my words.

His perfect mouth stretches into a wide grin. "Hardly. And by the looks of those red splotches on your neck, something tells me you don't even believe your own words."

I did not expect him to best me in my snarky comment, so my mouth pops open like a fish out of water, making his smile bigger, then he shrugs.

"I, uh... well... I..." Never has someone rendered me speechless before, but this local hottie has done it in thirty seconds flat. I'm both infuriated and impressed.

He gives his head a slow shake as he turns to open the door to his truck.

Right when I'm about to retrieve my tongue from my throat, a lady yells, "Yoo-hoo."

I turn to see her across the parking lot, sitting in a lounge chair next to a wooden stand. She holds her big floppy hat on her head with one hand as she waves me over with the other. "Hey there. You look like you could use some homemade treats."

Not really. Her pies and cookies are calling my name anyway, though. Over my shoulder, I do a girly wave and say to the guy, "Have a nice day."

As I walk toward the lady, I feel the burn of his stare. Before I can reach the lady's stand, he peels out of the gas station. *Yep, over-compensating.*

She waves to him, and he waves back. Then she asks, "Do you see anything you like, other than Mitch, that is?"

"What?"

The elderly lady lets out a smoky laugh. "He sure is mighty fine to look at, even for an old codger like me."

Very uncomfortable with this conversation, I focus on the items on the table. "Do you have anything without nuts?"

The lady scrunches up her nose. "In the middle of a pecan field?"

"Peck-cans?"

The lady points to the bag of pecans, and now my itchy throat makes sense. "Oh, I'm sorry. I think I'll have to pass."

As I walk away, she yells, "Don't buy from Mary Sue in Ocilla. Her stuff is store-bought with a new label slapped on the jar."

"Thank you for the tip. Have a nice day."

I slide back into my perfectly sized car and drive until, like an oasis in the desert, a sign appears, announcing, "Welcome to Smithville." From the rust around the edges, I'm thinking the sign has been up as long as the city has been in existence. As I drive down Main Street, several people wave at me. I wave back and remember Penny telling me people like to do that in small towns. "It's just a natural act—not like they want something from you," she said.

I pull into the empty parking lot of the Peach Fuzz Inn, and I'm not surprised by the establishment. It's not much more than a Motel Six with a big peach for the sign that rotates, I guess to make sure all visitors to this fine town know they are open for business. The weeds popping up throughout the asphalt say otherwise.

Stepping into the lobby with luggage in tow, I'm surrounded by peach everything—peach wallpaper, peach candles, pens with peaches on the pen caps—and to the side of the lobby is a small souvenir shop that looks like a peach exploded in there. The rack of T-shirts hanging near the entrance of the store has an enormous peach on the front that reads Made in Georgia. *That's got to be a best seller.* I spot some souvenir teacups and make a mental note to pick one up for my mother. They aren't vintage, but she loves anything unusual.

I ring the bell, and a man that could be Joe Dirt's twin brother enters from the office behind the counter. He grins, holding a toothpick between his teeth. "May I help you, ma'am?"

"Ma'am" usually has one, maybe two, syllables, but this guy added about four more just for good measure, just like big-truck dude did.

"Yes, I have a reservation. Jackie Myers."

Using his index fingers, he types into a computer similar to the one I had in grade school. "M... E..."

"*M, Y, E, R, S*. Myers. First name is Jackie." No one here has to know Myers is my middle name.

"I got a cousin named Jackie. He's a boy. I'm Bobby James, by the way. BJ for short."

"That's nice. And it's nice to meet you."

He hands me the key chain, a plastic diamond shape with the number 208 on it. "You're on the second floor, just to the right. I think you'll like that one. Not too much morning sun, and it overlooks a nice patch of crepe myrtles. That's the room I reserve when my mother-in-law comes to visit." He leans over and whispers, "Anything is better than her staying in the same house as me."

"I bet." I take the key then glance around. "Thank you. Should I leave my luggage here for the valet?"

"Valet? We don't have a valet, but if you need help, I can take them up there for you."

Penny mentioned I would have to tamp down my independence for a few days because men down here tend to have manners, and it would be an insult if I were too hard-nosed.

"Sure. Thank you."

As he walks up the stairs to my room, he says, "You came in town at just the right time. The fall festival is this weekend. Lots of good eats, bouncy castle, good music, and dancin'." He motions with his head down the stairs. "Just take the sidewalk to the main square, or follow your nose." He takes in a deep breath. "I can't wait to get me some funnel cake. Have you had funnel cake?"

I shake my head.

"You got to try some funnel cake. I've never been able to make me a good funnel cake, but they are mm-mm-good at the festival." He rubs his stomach for added effect.

"Thanks for the tip."

"And the best part is you get to taste test all sorts of goodies and vote for your favorite." He looks off with a dazed expression and adds, "I always have a hard time choosing between Carla Ryan's chess pie and Mrs. McDonald's apple pecan dump cake. Mmm."

I do a full-body shiver as I unlock my room, which is peach scented. *Shocker.*

He sets my luggage down and backs out of the room. "I'll let you get settled. Welcome to Smithville."

Before I can offer him a tip, he trots down the stairs. In Atlanta, a bellhop would be standing there with his hand out, waiting for cash to be given and not leave until he has something to show for his help.

My room is a complete one-eighty from the outside of the building. The four-poster bed has a massive, cream-colored comforter on it, a slight shade lighter than the walls. Artwork, which looks original, hangs over the bed, and a smaller piece with a similar lake theme is next to the rolltop desk. Even the hardwood floors look well-kept, and the throw rugs have enough color in them to offset the neutral colors. But the cherry on the top is the balcony. I open the doors, and although the view is nothing more than one of the lazy streets below, I feel like a princess looking down from my window in a castle, minus the prince, of course. This is definitely a nice surprise, and I look forward to taking a well-deserved nap in that massive bed.

But first, I need a hot shower to revive me from a long road trip. Maybe after that, I'll take Bobby James's advice and stroll down Main Street to see what this sleepy little town has to offer. It will help me in my assessment of how much this town really needs its own hospital. After being cooped up in my car all day, a nice, leisurely walk will do me some good. *Perhaps I'll meet some more quaint town folk while I'm out. I just hope I don't get lost.*

CHAPTER FOUR
Mitch

Clint follows me in his G-Wagon to Silas's house to help me pack my scant belongings. In my mind, my interaction with the sharp-tongued redhead keeps playing in a loop. I hope she got her toy car's tank filled up and skedaddled out of town to irritate the next poor soul. But man, she was gorgeous with all those curves and perfect smile. She could seriously make me forget all my troubles in a New York minute, and I have to admit to myself that it's nice to have some new scenery for a change, even for just a moment.

When we open the front door, Clint is bombarded by two sets of arms and legs from our tiny nephews. Since he's been back home, they have taken to him like ducks to water.

"Unc Clint," Caleb says, swinging from Clint's bicep. Carson runs in circles around my brother's legs.

"Hey now, I thought I was your favorite uncle." I catch Carson as he makes another rotation around his new favorite uncle. He lets out a giggle when I tickle his stomach.

Marlo enters, carrying her newborn daughter. "You know they love you too. They're just making up for lost time."

I caress baby Chloe's tiny foot between my fingers before I take her from her mother's arms. "That's okay. I'll be over here, smooching on my favorite niece." Chloe's smooth cheeks feel like soft dough, and oh man, I'll never get enough of that newborn smell. Chloe's head bobbles around until she's settled in my arms, and her little body nestled up against mine makes me almost forget how craptastic my day has been so far.

I take in Marlo's appearance. She always looks a little frazzled when dealing with the twins, but now, she looks as if she could fall asleep standing up. At that exact moment, Chloe spews a foul sour-milk liquid all over her onesie.

Marlo whimpers, and tears form in her eyes. "I just changed her clothes two minutes ago."

I need to talk to Clint about hiring her some help. Three children under the age of three is wearing her out. "I've got this. Clint will be the monkey bars for a few minutes, and I'll get this little girl all sweet smelling again. You rest on the couch."

I don't have to tell her twice. Before I can leave the living room, Marlo has her feet up on the coffee table, head tilted back as she wipes tears of exhaustion from her face.

"Come on, Sweet C. Let's make you presentable again."

As I enter my room, which doubles as Chloe's nursery, I hear the muffled ruckus from the living room. I love my nephews more than words can describe, but there's something special about this baby girl. I place her on the changing table and pull out all the supplies to change her clothes, and upon further inspection, she could use a dry diaper, as well.

"Sweet C, how are you able to make such a pukey mess?"

With knees pulled up to her chest, it's a challenge to strap on a fresh diaper and slide four tiny appendages inside the holes of her clean onesie. When I'm done, I feel the tiniest of victories, like I've roped a calf at the county fair.

"There. Feeling better?"

I hold her with her head on my shoulder and sink down into the glider to have a little quiet time with this angel. She and I have had some great moments in the last month, and she's helped me solve a bunch of problems.

"C, it's time I find my own place to live so I can sort out my life, but it's not because of anything you've done. Don't tell your brothers, but you're my favorite."

Chloe lifts her wobbly head, turns the other direction, and plops it down again. The rhythmic glider puts me in a quiet zone, and I could stay like this forever. Silas and Marlo would let me continue to live with them, but I'm ready to move on.

Caleb screeches at the top of his lungs while Carson chases him down the hallway. Clint, right on their heels, has a wild but happy expression on his face. Now that he and Regina have reunited, it won't surprise me if I have a few more nieces or nephews in the near future. Then all of them will call me their single uncle.

Caleb runs back down the hallway, and as soon as he steps over the threshold of my room-slash-nursery, it's like he's a totally different kid. He places a hand over his mouth and tiptoes toward me and the baby. Once he gets to us, he kisses her hand, turns on a dime, and tiptoes out of the room. When he gets to the door, he morphs back into a screeching banshee. The twins may be out of control most times, but Marlo laid down the law about respecting Chloe's sleep space.

I nuzzle into Chloe's baby-fine hair and kiss the top of her head. As much as I want to stay in this newborn-fresh bubble for the rest of my life, I know it's not the right thing to do, so I place her in her bassinet and turn on the infant monitor. The floor creaks when Clint enters the room.

In a hushed tone, he says, "You're a natural with babies."

"You pick up a thing or two when you're surrounded by them."

"Looks good on you. Need a hand getting your stuff?"

"There's not much to get. Mostly just some clothes and my laptop. I live pretty lean."

He pulls a duffel bag from under the bed and stuffs clothes from the dresser into it. "I hear you about lean living. I pretty much owned underwear and a coffee pot while I was playing ball."

Clint used to be a professional baseball player, but he gave it all up to come back to Smithville. I think he's crazy, but a part of me really gets it. Love can make a person do irrational things. Not that I know anything about love. The closest thing I had to love was my affection toward Mel, and it's clear that was all a waste of time.

Breaking my fog, Clint says, "You'll like the studio apartment above In a Jam. It's small, but..." He waves a T-shirt around the room. "It's bigger than this."

"My truck is bigger than this." I suck in a breath and mumble, "I hope Marlo didn't hear me. I'd never want to hurt her feelings. She's been so kind to let me live here all these years."

"She'd never turn you away. I won't either."

"Thanks, bro."

He lets out a chuckle and looks over his shoulder before he pulls something out of my bottom drawer. Clint dangles a pack of condoms in my face, and I snatch them out of his grip.

"Hoping you'd get lucky?"

I bury them in the bottom of the duffel bag as my ears burn from embarrassment. "It never hurts to hope, but I should check the expiration dates on those things. I'm sure they're useless by now."

I lean down to give Chloe a soft kiss to the top of her head and whisper, "Remember, I'm your favorite uncle."

"I heard that." Clint slings my bag over his shoulder. I pick up my laptop bag, and a sudden pang of sadness hits me. My life is nothing more than two bags. Surely after all this time, I should have more to show for myself. Heck, I hardly have anything in the bank either.

As if he can read my mind, Clint shrugs. "Who needs a bunch of stuff anyway?"

"Yeah," I reply. "I guess you're right."

Since reality hit me right in the balls, it kick-started my newfound attitude on life. I'm done wasting time on people who are not emotionally available. The new and improved Mitch is going to look out for himself, and he certainly won't fall for anyone anytime soon.

CHAPTER FIVE
Jackie

After I shower the travel funk off my body, I sink into the mattress and moan in delight. When I close my eyes, I do my best to plan out my first action step for the hospital, but all my mind focuses on is the gas station hottie with the pale-blue eyes that sparkled when he smiled. That grin was infectious. Not to mention how nice he filled out those jeans. And his banter... If I weren't down here on business, I would have followed him to wherever he was going.

Actually, I can dream I would do something like that, but I never do anything spontaneous. I research, set objectives, determine a plan of action, then implement the plan. It even took me three weeks to determine if I was getting the best deal for my Mini Cooper, and that was after the four months it took to decide on what car to buy. So, as much as I want to fantasize about following some random dude, I know I would never follow through with that.

I shake my head to clear away all the whimsical ideas. This visit requires my complete attention—my advancement depends on it. So I give my hormones a good, stern talking-to, just to show them who's in control. There is just not enough time in the day to have it all, and right now, I want that promotion more than I want anything else, even a six-foot-tall, hot slice of pizza.

My phone buzzes, notifying me of a text, and I let out a whimper as I rise from the comfy bed to read the text from my father: *So proud of you.*

I fire off a quick thanks and go to the closet to find some presentable, but casual clothes to wear while touring this little town.

Smithville needs to really convince me they need the hospital, because the data is telling me otherwise.

When I descend the stairs to the main area of the inn, I find Bobby James behind the front desk, reading what looks to be a paperback romance novel. When he sees me, he slams the book closed and shoves it in a drawer. With a sheepish grin, he says, "I found that in one of the rooms, and I was looking to see if the owner put her name in it."

"Or *his* name. You never know."

He scratches the back of his head.

"I like Jessica McFarland's novels, but if you get a chance, you should check out Sarah Slade's." I stare at the ceiling and sigh. "I hear *Lords of Love* is supposed to be her best yet."

"That's what I heard," he yells then clears his throat. "I mean, uh... really? I'll have to tell my wife about that one."

I wink. "You do that. So, Bobby James, will I get lost if I take a walk?"

He guffaws. "Not at all. Just head down the sidewalk and mosey around the square. You'll end up back here. Oh, and don't forget about the festival tomorrow. You don't want to miss it."

With a wave and a thank you, I leave the inn to see what Smithville has to offer. This is exactly what I need to relinquish work stress. I don't remember a day in the last five years when I took a walk, just for the sake of getting some fresh air. If I'm able to fit anything physical into my normal day, it's usually only twenty minutes on my Peloton bike. The smoggy air in the city, combined with the fear of getting mugged, always kept me safely tucked inside my apartment on the twentieth floor.

But today, I saunter down the sidewalk with no agenda. People wander around, greeting others with a smile or a wave. I overhear a lady ask another lady, "How's your mama?" Then she babbles on and on about what her mother is up to.

I slide down onto a park bench to watch what life is like in Smithville. When my phone rings, I check my watch and know before

I even answer who the caller is. My sister, Gretta, always calls at five o'clock to give me the daily scoop on how her day was so stressful, wrangling her kids, the parent-teacher meeting, tennis lessons, and a yoga class. Every day, she reminds me how lucky I am that I don't have kids so I can focus on my career.

"Hey, Gretta."

"Well, Dad called twice to brag about your promotion."

"I don't have it yet."

She snorts. "You're up against bratty Brett, so I can safely say it's in the bag. He's not the most competent person in the company."

I roll my eyes, even though I know she can't see me. "Tell me about it. Do you remember that science project in high school? I had to redo all of his parts because he kept using mixing up 'their' and 'there.' I have no idea how he got through law school. He's not stupid, but he doesn't pay attention to the details."

"And you're the 'leave no stone unturned' kind of person, so yeah, you'll get the promotion."

"I hope so."

A tall, thin lady with a cigarette hanging out of her mouth walks past. She smiles as she passes me, and I catch myself smiling back.

Gretta sighs. "You know how Dad goes overboard about his praise for you. You deserve it, but I wish he would get past the fact that I quit my job to be a stay-at-home mom."

I can still hear my father saying, "I paid all that money for you to go to law school, and you're going to give it up to change diapers and run a carpool?" The hurt on my sister's face is still vivid in my mind. It's not easy for a woman to have it all, and I know Gretta doesn't regret her choice, at least when the kids are behaving.

"Judge Dalton only sees things as black or white. Your kids are awesome, and I don't ever remember a time when he shied away from bragging about them. And lots of professional women have fulfilling careers and a great home life. But it is harder for a woman."

"True, but I'm so exhausted most of the time, and I got roped into coordinating the Halloween parties for Breckenridge *and* Katie. How can I do two parties at the same time? I wish I could duplicate myself so I can be at two places at once." She groans then adds her daily comment, "You're so lucky you don't have kids." Gretta gasps. "I didn't mean it to come out like that. I love my kids to the moon and back, but if it weren't for my nanny, I would never be able to be so involved in the community and my kids' school activities."

Stretching my legs out in front of me, I watch two elderly ladies walk down the sidewalk across the street. One sneers while the other one holds her phone out like she's taking a picture of me. "If there's anyone who's up to the challenge, it's certainly you."

Gretta sighs in an overly dramatic way. "That's enough about me. Did you make it to your work site?"

"If by 'work site' you mean Smithville, then yes, I did make it. Took me twice as long with all the traffic jams, but I'm here now. And I'm actually sitting on a park bench in the middle of town, enjoying the fresh air, and it is surprisingly very relaxing."

"You don't have anything valuable on you, do you?"

"First off, no. I do not. Secondly, it really appears to be quite safe here." Glancing around, I notice people going about their business, laughing and smiling. A small child toddles down the sidewalk ten feet ahead of his mother, who appears to feel no sense of urgency to snatch him up before some creepy person kidnaps him.

"Looks can be deceiving. Just be careful, okay?"

I laugh. "Be careful about what? That I may not run through all my antacids in one day?"

"Careful that you might like it too much down there. Keep your eye on the prize."

"Eye on the prize, sister." I stand and continue my walk, passing cute shops with catchy names—In a Jam, Big Ash Fitness, Carpet Diem, and Back to the Fuchsia Flowers. They're all so quaint without being too corny, except for the Big Ash Fitness. Even I can see the play on words, and it reminds me my big ash needs a good workout.

"Did you hear anything I said?" Gretta asks.

Not having a clue to what my sister said, I reply, "I think you should do some retail therapy."

"I love the way you think."

"I'm really tired, so I'll call you later, okay?"

Before she has a chance to go into another round of complaints, I disconnect the call and continue walking down the street. I stop in front of the shop called In a Jam. Even with the wonky awning over the door and the faded painted sign on the window, this shop calls to me. Looking inside, I notice an elderly lady and a young woman about my age behind the counter. The lady must have said something funny, because the younger one doubles over with giggles.

I continue all the way around the block, and my throat is parched. Without a coffee shop anywhere in sight, I narrow my options as to which store might have something to drink. Once I get back to that jam shop, I'll have to see if they have anything to quench my thirst.

CHAPTER SIX

Mitch

When Andie sees us enter In a Jam, she holds out her arms wide. "Hey there, my new tenant."

I immediately feel at home.

Clint grins as he gestures to Mrs. Cavanaugh. "Sorry I bailed on you so soon, but a better offer came up." He waggles his eyebrows, making Andie squeal.

I toss my bags into the back booth. "Andie, I really appreciate you letting me stay here. I'll pay you whatever the going rate is."

She snaps a dishtowel at me, popping me on the leg. "The going rate is zero dollars, plus watching out for Mrs. Cavanaugh. She worries me being here so early all by herself."

"I can do that. I'm used to getting up early anyway. I only hope I don't get in the way."

"Nonsense." Mrs. Cavanaugh shuffles around the counter to embrace me. "I'm looking forward to having the Smithville Stud living under this roof. It will be good for business."

Clint belts out a laugh, and I smack him in the stomach. That nickname stuck many years ago, and I've never been able to shake it. I wish people appreciated my brain as much as they love the exterior. I work hard to stay in shape, and I can't help it if I look just like my father, who was a handsome dude—that is, before he got hooked on meth. I would rather be known for being kind and smart, though.

Mrs. Cavanaugh shakes a bony finger in my face. "You better eat the leftovers every night. I don't like wasting food. Do you understand?"

"Yes, ma'am, I do, and that will not be a problem. I stay hungry."

"You stay hawt too."

Andie gasps and turns Mrs. Cavanaugh around to shoo her back behind the counter. "Mrs. Cavanaugh, that was mighty forward of you."

She snorts. "Truth hurts. Now, I don't want you parading a bunch of skanky women up here. Do you hear me?"

"I promise I won't." I want to clarify that it would never happen, but I'd rather finish this uncomfortable conversation as fast as possible, so I leave it at that. "Actually, I was hoping you would let me use the shop's kitchen."

Mrs. Cavanaugh rubs her hands together. "Ooh, is it what I think it is?"

A flush begins to creep up my neck, but I am proud of the one dessert I can make. "It is. Would you help me?"

"Like white on rice."

The bells over the front door chime, and we all turn to stare at the stranger darkening the door of In a Jam. She has striking long auburn hair and wears one of those gauzy type shirts that slips off her left shoulder and faded skin-tight jeans that show off her curves. Her sunglasses almost cover her entire apple-shaped face. *Damn, she's gorgeous.*

When I recognize it's the Mini Cooper lady, my eyes narrow. "Oh, it's you."

She slides her sunglasses to rest on top of her head to reveal melt-in-your-mouth brown eyes as her head snaps back when she sees me. With a chin held high, she replies, "Hey there, heart-stopper."

"What are you doing here?"

She quirks up her eyebrow. "Work. And you?"

I feel everyone's eyes in the shop on me. "I happen to live here."

Her eyebrows form a V in confusion.

Clearing my throat, I say, "Well, not here, but..." I point to the ceiling. "Up there. So yeah. Here." I don't know why I feel the need to explain my living situation to her, but the more I talk, the lamer it sounds.

We have a staring competition for a long moment, neither of us saying anything else, until Andie breaks the silence. "Welcome to In a Jam. What can I get for you?"

The salty lady snaps her head toward Andie and turns on a heart-stopping smile. "Can I see a menu?"

A menu?

Clint slides her a laminated menu that I doubt has been updated since the seventies. I glance toward Andie, and she just shrugs at me.

Tapping her finger to her chin, the redhead mulls over the choices, which are scant. "Do you have chai tea?"

I chuckle, and in a girly voice, I say, "Chai tea?"

When she turns her attention back to me with the fierceness of a thousand suns, I swallow my laughter. "Do you work here?"

"No, ma'am, it's just that—"

She holds a hand out in front of my face, and I immediately swallow the rest of my sentence.

Under his breath, Clint mumbles, "Bro, she put you in your place."

She points her finger at Clint. "I know you from somewhere."

I let out a groan. Of course she would hone in on him. "You said you wouldn't bring your groupies to town when you moved back."

She gasps. "I am *not* a groupie. I'm here on business."

"Really? What kind?"

Mrs. Cavanaugh shushes me, but I puff out my chest.

The stranger takes two steps toward me, rolls her eyes, then turns her attention back to Andie and Mrs. Cavanaugh. "I'd like a very large glass of sweet tea, please."

"Coming right up." Andie fills the glass with ice while Clint and I slink into a booth to avoid the stranger's wrath.

"I'm Andie, by the way, and this is Mrs. Cavanaugh. She's my business partner. I own the building, and she runs the shop."

"Nice to meet you. You don't sound like you're from around here."

Andie blushes. "Guilty. I'm a transplant. Moved here not long ago, and I fell in love with the place."

"Or the man," Mrs. Cavanaugh adds.

"That too. I'm from Boston. You?"

The stranger sips her tea then replies, "Atlanta."

From the booth, I add, "No one is *from* Atlanta. They're from somewhere else and moved there."

She swings around on the stool and stalks toward me like a cheetah about to devour her prey. It's a combination of terrifying and thrilling.

Clint lets out an "Uh-oh" as she plops down in the booth next to him. He scoots as far away from the human tornado as possible.

"For the record, I was born at Northside Hospital and grew up in Druid Hills."

"Ah," I say, looking at Clint. "Snooty Hills."

She stares at the ceiling and chuckles. "You know nothing about me. I just stopped in to this lovely shop, and all you do is throw barbs my way." She glances over at Clint. "He even insulted my car."

Clint turns to me. "What kind of car does she drive?"

"One of those Matchbox-looking models."

"Does it have a wind-up key?"

"Probably."

She drums her fingers on the table as she waits for us to finish. "And another thing—I am *not* snooty."

"Of course you aren't."

"Is this how you treat all visitors to Smithville?" She glances around the room, but no one speaks.

After a pause, I dare to reply to her comment. "We don't get many visitors. I think Andie was the last one."

Andie does a one-shoulder shrug as she checks her receipts for the day.

Miss Brown Eyes snaps her fingers and turns her attention to Clint. "The Braves. That's where I know you from. You're Clint Sorrow."

His cheeks turn red. "I may have played for the Braves, but I'm not *from* Atlanta."

I shake my head. "Didn't you say that one time on an interview? I specifically remember someone asking you early on in your career where you were from, and you said Atlanta."

Clint runs his fingers through his hair. "That was a long time ago." He gazes over at the stranger and adds, "I'm retired."

"And engaged," Mrs. Cavanaugh adds from the counter. "But the Smithville Stud across from him is very available."

I cringe at her words.

The stranger's gaze ping-pongs around the room, and when she lands on mine again, she asks, "Is it always this exciting in Smithville?"

Her words could not be laced with more sarcasm if she tried. Holding her stare long enough for her to lose contact first, I feel a small victory.

From across the booth, Clint smacks me in the arm. "Always something happening here. I'm Clint, and this is my brother, Mitch. We're lifers here in Smithville. How long are you here for?"

"Long enough to get my job done."

The stranger, who can throw barbs as well she takes them, swallows the last sip of her tea, stands, and deposits the empty glass on the counter. She fishes out a ten-dollar bill and slides it toward Andie. "Keep the change."

Before she gets to the door, Andie says, "I didn't get your name."

She turns and glares at me before speaking. "Jackie. Jackie Myers."

"Welcome to Smithville, Jackie," Andie says. "Will we see you this weekend at the fall festival? It's supposed to be a big hit."

"So I've been told. I might have to check it out. Any chance one of you would be kind enough to point me in the direction of Smithville Regional Hospital?"

All eyes turn toward me. My Spidey senses kick in, and I'm not sure why. "What for? You planning on being admitted while you're here? We won't give you food poisoning, if that's what you're worried about."

"Nope. Not where I was headed with that. I am..." She swallows and takes a deep breath. "I'm doing a story on the town and want to include a section on the hospital."

Clint turns to me. "I hear there's a fine staff there, you know, just in case."

I kick my brother's foot.

"Ouch."

Her eyes dance with amusement, causing my pulse to throb in my ears. *Talk about a heart-stopper.* Then, one by one, she points at us. "Goodbye, Mrs. Cavanaugh, Andie, Clint, and... the Stud." With that, she leaves.

Clint collapses over the table in a fit of laughter. "Dude, if you could see your face right now."

I shake my head. "Whatever, man, I'm going to settle in upstairs if y'all don't mind."

Clint shakes his head. "Not at all. And I'll bring you some chai tea as a housewarming present."

Laughter fills the café as I make my way up the stairs to my new home. Clint's harassment is nothing I'm not used to, but something is up with the redhead. I'm not sure how she can be so gorgeous and yet incredibly intimidating at the same time. That combination makes her intriguing and dangerous.

No one just comes to Smithville for work. There is no work to travel to. She's up to something, and it can't be good.

I stare at my new apartment, and I already know I'm going to like living here. It has a nice big window overlooking the main square of the city, and it feels homey. It's a small studio apartment, but I couldn't ask for more at this stage in my life. I can kick back, watch a football game, and eat whenever and whatever I want without little kids in my lap, stealing my food and wanting to change the channel to the Disney Channel. Just thinking about them makes me already miss the daylights out of them. They may be rascals, but I love them just the way they are.

But the best part of having this space is I can have friends over if I want without feeling like I'm creating more of a mess for my sister-in-law. *Guy friends, of course. I'm done with women for a very long time.*

Mrs. Cavanaugh has nothing to worry about. There will be no skanky women darkening the door of this apartment. In fact, there won't be *any* women coming here for a very, very long time—if ever.

CHAPTER SEVEN

Jackie

After I ordered a burger from Beefcakes, I sacked out for the night. Way before my alarm is set to go off, I'm wide awake, thinking about my altercation with the Smithville Stud—or if I caught his name correctly, Mitch. I never expected to see him again, and he caught me off guard when he was in the shop. Of all places for me to wander into and he lives above it. For a moment, I was stunned, staring at that face and those shoulders. And those smiley eyes. *Gah!*

I need to give myself a good, stern talking-to for checking out his butt when he sauntered over to the booth. And I hate to admit to myself how much I enjoyed our little banter session. The room was heating up, and it certainly wasn't because of the oven. Even with Penny's warning about how "they" grow them down here, I was not prepared for *him.* When he started giving me crap about my car again and how he gave as much as he took, it was a bit of a turn-on. He seems to know the right buttons to push to get me riled, and I definitely felt the need to rise to the occasion. Even if he's a fine specimen, he's kind of broody, too, like he carries a lot of baggage. I should steer clear of that.

Just as my eyes begin to close again, my phone buzzes. I let out a whimper, because I do not want to talk to anyone about any subject—work, family, anything. The buzzing continues, so I grab the phone off the nightstand and see that it's Brett calling me. I think I would have enjoyed a conversation with my sister more than *him.* At least my family does most of the talking and all I have to do is interject an occasional "uh-huh" every now and then. But Brett loves to get under my skin. He's been that way ever since we were young, with his uncanny ability to know when I'm the most frustrated. I wouldn't put it past him to have my phone bugged so he knows when to pounce. But knowing my pain-in-the-butt colleague, he won't stop calling until I answer the phone.

"What?" I answer.

"Good morning to you, too, Sunshine. I'm just sitting in the Cypress Bed and Breakfast, sipping my iced caramel macchiato, watching the mimosa trees sway in the breeze. It's lovely here."

"Such a manly drink, but I'm not surprised. Is that all you called for?"

"Just checking to see if you got settled in."

"Why do you care?"

"My room is a palace. Huge bed. Massive en suite with a Jacuzzi. Yeah... I'm definitely going to make good use of that."

Ew. I hope it gets disinfected after he leaves.

"Tell me about *your* room."

Scanning my small room, I say, "It's cozy, surprisingly clean, and... very peachy."

He snorts, and I want to crawl through the phone and give him a titty twister.

"Did I mention that Tifton is a college town? Yes... gorgeous site. Young women everywhere."

"You're too old for that crowd."

"Young ladies are attracted to slightly older men with a hefty bank account."

"And a hefty beer belly? Look, if you don't have anything else to bore me with, I need to go. I have lots to prepare for tomorrow."

After silence on the other end of the phone, he says, "You're not starting work before Monday, are you?"

I wish. "I have a fall festival to attend this weekend."

"Yee-haw."

"You're missing the point, as usual. It's the perfect opportunity to hobnob with the locals. I bet I'll fit right in."

"Kind of like a toaster in a bathtub?"

He sends me a photo of three college-aged girls wearing barely anything. I delete it immediately.

"I need to let you go."

"Fine, Mr. Perv. What do you have planned to obtain intel?"

"I'm going to a uni football game." He sighs. "Just like old times."

"Don't do any keg stands. Your thirtyish soft belly will be the quickest way to turn off the ladies."

He knows I speak the truth. Last year, at the company picnic, he was on the "skins" team for Frisbee football, and I was almost blinded. He must wear a girdle to work, because there is no way he could hold that gut in for eight hours a day.

"Harrumph. Penny likes my body, and you know it."

"Ew. I just threw up in my mouth. And if by 'likes' you mean 'is disgusted by,' then you would be correct. And I'm using her words. Leave Penny out of it. Trust me, she could probably kick your butt into next week."

"She's in denial. Keep me posted on how things go in your 'neck of the woods.'" His terrible attempt at a Southern accent would get him punched in the face if he were really here.

"College kids are not going to know the first thing about the hospital."

His silence speaks volumes. I should have just let him sink on his own. As much fun as he's having gawking at young skirts, it's not going to help his cause. I stare at the ceiling and mentally give myself a kick in the butt. "And as usual, you can send me your proposal so I can proof it for grammatical errors."

"Ha. You want to sabotage it, don't you?"

I may be competitive and want this promotion more than anything else in the world, but I'm not vindictive. "Fine. Don't send it."

He growls. "I'll email it to you by midweek."

A *whoop* sound outside draws my attention out my window. "Gotta go," I say then hang up before he has a chance to respond.

Opening my balcony door, I step outside. I notice a shirtless guy poking his head inside the window of a police car across the street from the bed-and-breakfast. His butt and muscular legs are all that's visible from my vantage point. Not that I'm complaining. He backs away from the car and does a knuckle bump with the driver. The shirtless guy exposes a nice V shape of shoulders to abs. He's chiseled like Hercules. *Purrr.*

My buzz fades when I realize who he is. "You've got to be kidding me." It's the Stud. He's like a bad penny, showing up everywhere without warning.

The policeman points a finger in my direction, and I know the exact moment when Mitch notices me standing on the balcony, because his movie-star-perfect smile morphs into a snarl. The policeman hits his siren for a quick toot, then he drives away. Shaking his head, Mitch stuffs his earbuds into his ears then runs down the sidewalk.

My mind goes back to the bumper sticker on his truck. *Cute enough to stop your heart. Skilled enough to revive it.* There is no doubt in my mind that he works at the hospital in some capacity, and I can't believe I didn't pick up on that when I first saw it.

As I watch him turn a corner, I sling on my running shoes. While I'm here, I might as well enjoy the scenery. It doesn't cost to look as long as I don't touch. Plus, if I turn on the charm, maybe he will give me some valuable information for my report.

Bobby James is dusting the furniture in the front room of the inn when I stumble down the stairs.

"Morning, Miss Myers."

"Good morning, Bobby James. That burger was delicious. Thanks for the recommendation."

He stuffs the dusting cloth into his back pocket and grins. "They always give our customers a discount, but I would suggest them if they charged double."

"Can I ask you a question?"

"Sure."

"From my window, I saw some people jogging that way." I point in the direction Mitch headed. Bobby James doesn't have to know that "people" is really one specific person.

He glances in the direction I pointed, and he nods. "Yeah, if you turn that corner and just keep going, you'll run right into the high school. Most people do laps around the football field."

"Thank you."

I wave to Bobby James then jog down the sidewalk in an attempt to work off the burger I ate last night. At least that's what I'm telling myself.

CHAPTER EIGHT
Mitch

Gunnar's aggravating chuckle rings in my ears as I move at a nice clip toward the high school track. A good run will help remove Miss Sexy Brown Eyes from my memory.

Shocked that I have the track to myself, I fall into a comfortable stride, getting lost in my thoughts. After three laps around the football field, I pick up the pace as sprinklers shoot water across the grass in preparation for the county championship game next Friday. Feeling a stitch in my side coming on, I slow down to a leisurely jog, consumed by the Southern rock tunes blasting through my earbuds.

When I round the end zone, I notice someone standing by the bleachers, stretching their quads. As I get closer, Jackie, of all people, flashes a smile, but I focus on the ground. My heart picks up the pace even if my feet don't.

She waves, and I snatch my earbuds out of my ears.

"Mind if I join you?"

"Harrumph. It's a free country. Try to keep up." Ignoring my screaming lungs, I pick up the pace. In my peripheral vision, I notice she's right next to me.

"That shouldn't be a problem. I ran cross country in high school *and* college."

"Figures." My hopes of her being allergic to exercise fade into the background. She falls into step next to me, her auburn hair slapping her in the face with every stride. Her breaths are in sync with mine.

"In case you didn't catch it yesterday, I'm Jackie Myers."

It's not polite to lie, so instead of saying "Nice to meet you," I just nod.

"Mitch, if I remember correctly. Your brother mentioned your name."

My stride lengthens, and it takes a couple of seconds until she catches up to me. Then, without warning, she turns up the speed. Before I register what's happening, she's a good fifteen feet ahead of me. There's no way I'm going to let this aggravating cuss of a woman get the best of me, so I take off at a sprint, catching her and whizzing past.

"Is that all you got, Stud?" she yells as she catches up to me.

We run another lap side by side, and her calm, steady breaths make it seem like no more than a walk in the park for her. I'm over here about to cough up a lung, though, which pisses me off.

I screech to a halt and bend at the waist, gasping for air, with my back to her.

Jackie stops running, walks toward me, then jogs in place. "You shouldn't suddenly stop. It's not good for—"

"I know that." I turn my back on her and walk with my hands over my head, doing my best to calm my breathing to a more normal rate.

When I can talk and breathe at the same time, I ask, "You following me?"

She comes within a foot of me, and I can feel the heat radiating off her body as sweat glistens on her skin.

She grins, showing off perfect teeth. "Nonsense. It was on the Chamber of Commerce's website as one of the top ten attractions in Smithville."

I scoff as I stare up at the sky. "The chamber doesn't have a website." With my heart rate finally under control, I turn to walk away from her, but she catches up.

"Maybe it should." She spreads her arms wide, her left hand brushing across my chest as she makes a sweeping motion. I take a step to the side to avoid any more unintentional touching. In a journalistic voice, she adds, "Quaint and open, overlooking a massive green space that would give Piedmont Park a run for its money."

I stop on a dime and wipe my sweaty brow. She turns toward me and flashes a cocky grin.

"Myers, what are you up to?"

Jackie walks to me and holds her hands out in defense. "I'm just here to write an article for the Atlanta Journal about twenty-first-century small towns. You should be honored this community will get so much attention."

I walk away from her and say over my shoulder, "First off, I don't buy a word you say, and secondly, we don't *need* attention."

She latches on to my bicep, and it flexes at her touch. I glance over at her as she snatches her hand away. "You don't believe I'm writing a story?"

"Nope."

She stares at the track for a moment, nibbling on her full bottom lip, then snaps her head up, almost as if a new person is inhabiting her body. "It doesn't matter what you think, Mitch Sorrow."

I chuckle. "You remembered my last name too? How charming. Just keep it out of your article," I say, using air quotes to make sure she knows I think she's completely full of it. "Have a nice day, Myers."

Turning around, I jog toward the parking lot and down the road then walk back to In a Jam. Mrs. Cavanaugh said she would help me bake pies today, and it will be the best way to work off my frustrations. I wish I would stop allowing women to get under my skin.

AFTER MY MOTHER LEFT, it was every man for himself in our kitchen. In order to keep from starving, Clint and I tried each recipe in my mother's plastic box. The smoke alarm went off so much, Silas had to install it down the hallway. Silas can grill like nobody's business, and

Clint's specialty is anything with pasta in it, but I'm only able to make a meal that borders on edible, except for deserts. I can bake a mean pie, if I do say so myself.

Mrs. Cavanaugh pulls out every miniature pie pan she has in the shop and lines them up next to the stove. "What are you going to make today?"

I smack the dog-eared recipe card down on the counter. "This is a family recipe. I can trust you, right?" Of course I can, but I love to mess with her.

She runs her fingers across her mouth as if she's zipping her lips shut then pretends to throw the key behind her shoulder. She holds up a finger as she shuffles around the counter and toward the front door. She peeks outside.

"What are you doing?"

"Making sure the Jackson sisters aren't around. Their mouths are as floppy as their hoo-has."

That was an overshare. I shiver to get the thought out of my mind.

As we gather all the ingredients, she hums an old gospel hymn. She places the pecans from Silas's yard into a grinder to make a fine flour out of it. Running her fingers through the pecan flour, she grins. "This is the secret ingredient, isn't it?"

With a bashful grin, I say, "Yeah. One of the few memories of my mother was her making pie crusts out of pecans."

"Keep the good memories. Toss the rest in the crapper, child."

Mrs. Cavanaugh was around when my mother flew the coop and sent my dad spiraling out of control, landing him in prison for life. She heard all the rumors, which all turned out to be true, but she never once blamed any of us Sorrow kids for our parents' failings. In fact, she'd provided us many meals, saying, "I made too much and didn't want it to go to waste." That sweet woman didn't have a pot to pee in, but she always made sure we didn't go hungry.

"You ready?"

She rubs her hands together like she's seventeen instead of eighty. "Let's do this."

We create the pie crusts and line twenty-four small pie pans, and while they pre-bake, we make the filling.

With the skill of someone half her age, Mrs. Cavanaugh hand stirs the ingredients as the aroma of pie crusts fills the shop. "I love that smell."

"Um-um. Nothing better."

"I bought enough to make ninety-six small pies. Do you think that's overkill?"

She fingers the filling and smacks her lips as she does a taste test. "*Under*kill is more like it. This will definitely be a contender for the town's favorite pie this season. I guarantee it. And I won't have to stuff the ballots this year."

I belt out a laugh. It's like she's my adopted grandmother, and I love having her in my life.

"What do you think about that Jackie girl?" she asks, whipping the batter once more. Just like a grandmother, she's a bit on the meddling side.

Trying to act nonchalant, I shrug. "Haven't thought about her until you brought her up."

She takes the pie tins out of the oven and begins to spoon in the filling. "Do you think I'm blind? I saw the way she was drinking you up like a cold glass of lemonade on the Fourth of July." She points the spoon at me and adds, "And you couldn't take your eyes off of her."

"She was condescending."

"Only because you were an ass."

My head snaps back as I take in her words. "I was not. She started acting all hoity-toity. I don't like when people come here and diss my town. And then, when we were jogging—"

I snap my mouth closed in hopes she didn't catch my slip-up.

She chuckles as she proceeds to gently place the pans in the oven. "Child, the last person from out of town that darkened the streets of Smithville was Andie, and she didn't exactly start out on the right foot either. I remember how she expected Gunnar to pay for his meal in this shop. Ha. His money doesn't spend here. Never has and never will. But look at her now. She's as much a part of this town as you and me."

"That is different. Andie was forced to live among us and fell in love. This girl... She's up to something. I just don't know what it is yet."

"You think she's hawt."

The spoon falls from my hand and lands on my shoe, splattering my pants with pie filling. "I do not think she's... hot."

Liar. You think she's scorching hot.

"Yep. You think she's hot, and you like that she went toe to toe with you. Some men like meek women, but you like them smart and strong and... hawt."

I wipe my hands on a dish towel. "Please, don't."

She wags her bony index finger in my face. "I know you had your heart and hopes set on Melly, but that ship has sailed."

I blow out a breath. "I spent so many years..."

"Remember that old saying about when one door closes?"

I nod.

"Child, that door closed a long time ago, but you just kept banging on the door, hoping it would open, but it was the wrong door. Go find the right door, and if you have to, just bust through a window."

I smile. "Yes, ma'am. While the pie crusts are in the oven, I think I'll go upstairs for a moment, if you don't mind."

Right before the door shuts behind me, she adds, "She thinks you're hot too. Just saying."

Everything about Jackie is hot: her beautiful brown eyes, her curvy figure, and her quick retort. *So much for being done with women. I hope Jackie's door is bolted shut.*

CHAPTER NINE
Jackie

The second item in Penny's small-town orientation lecture includes food. According to her, not only does every food imaginable have to be swimming in oil, it also has to be deep fat fried. I notice fried pickles, fried jellybeans, and fried beer, and I have barely walked past the entrance to the festival. Wow, this town doesn't do things halfway. A variety of booths with people selling their arts and crafts line one side of the venue, and there is a lady selling painted teacups I know my mother would love. I make a mental note to revisit that one and the one selling beaded jewelry, but not before I find something decent to eat.

The aroma of hot grease is everywhere, and I feel my arteries closing up as I walk past the fourth booth. Country music fills the air, and people meander around while the children run wild with no parental supervision. My sister would have a panic attack if her kids were not glued to her side all the time while she complained about having to watch over them at the same time.

A slender lady with short blond hair walks up to me, a cigarette in hand. I recognize her from my walk around the town. "Hey there. I'm Liza Jane. Welcome to the festival."

She hands me a piece of card stock and a short pencil, like the ones at a mini-golf course. "I apologize if no one took the time to fill you in on the contest, but each year, the community votes on the tastiest dessert." She points to the page. "The scorecard has all the booths that are competing. By each item you taste test, you rank it. One being the worst and ten being the best." She leans close to me and stage-whispers, "Don't eat the Jacksons' Rocky Mountain oysters."

"Do they have nuts in them?"

Liza belts out a laugh. "You could say that. Hope to see you around town," she says as she takes a puff from her cigarette. "I gotta go find my old man. Nice to meet you."

"You too," I say to her retreating frame.

As I read the list of desserts, I immediately cross off three items I know better than to eat: toffee nut pie, utterly deadly Southern pecan tarts, and apple walnut Bundt cake. While I turn around in a circle to decide where to begin, two small boys careening out of control run into me, almost knocking me down. They giggle as they run past me in a flash.

"Caleb, Carson. Get back here," a pretty lady with a tiny infant in her arms yells. She stops to catch her breath when Mitch jogs up to her. *There he is again.*

She asks me, "Did you see which way they went?"

I point toward the dunking booth. "I think they went that way."

"Here." She hands the infant to Mitch, and he cuddles the baby like he's a pro. "I just changed her diaper, so she's good to go for a while."

Well, settles that. It's kind of odd for a married man with children to still be called the Stud, but whatever. He's definitely off-limits, which is a relief. It's also a little unusual that he lives above the shop. *Maybe they're having trouble and that's why he is so cranky.*

Mitch's lips graze the tiny baby's head. "It's you again."

"Yep, it's me. What a sweet baby you have there."

His hand caresses her back as he rocks back and forth. "Yes, she is." He plants a soft kiss on her tiny head, and my hormones surge throughout my body. Mitch's large arms are like a cocoon protecting her. There nothing sexier than a man loving on a baby.

I snap out of my nonsense, because it's kind of creepy of me to be gawking at a married man. "Your daughter is beautiful."

"She is." His eyes snap wide open. "Wait. My daughter? No. This is my niece, Chloe. Chloe, meet Jackie. She's a... journalist." He lowers his voice and says to Chloe, "We don't believe that, do we?" He puts his ear up to Chloe's face and nods. "She doesn't believe it either."

"Come on, Chloe. I bet your aunt Regina would like some cuddle time with you." He motions with his head and adds, "You should stop by booth number twelve and try my buttermilk pie. I think I might win this year."

I cock an eyebrow. "You bake?"

"When I'm not working or on baby duty." His nose crinkles up in disgust. "And with that, I really need to go."

"Don't forget to wash your hands," I yell, but he's gone.

Over his shoulder, he waves as he smooches on the baby's little cheek. Saying I watched him walk away with the swagger few men can pull off while carrying an infant would be putting it mildly. I one hundred percent gawked.

The men I'm surrounded by on a daily basis usually leave the child-raising to the mother. Matthew has pictures of his kids in his office, but I bet he never changed a poopy diaper or helped out with a middle-of-the-night feeding. Brett wouldn't know a binky from a burp cloth. But Mitch... I get the impression he would embrace all the mundane tasks of taking care of a child.

I need to find the dunk tank so I can douse the hormonal flames surging through my body right now. I'm here to work, not to get all hot and bothered about babies, men, and men with babies.

I return to my search for food and end up with a funnel cake, which is surprisingly quite tasty. I stop at every booth because I want to get the full small-town-festival experience. The bright colors of one tent lure me toward it. The sign Knit Picky swings in the breeze. A young lady and a small child tend to a table filled with all sorts of knitted toys. I quickly take a photo of the booth with my phone.

"Hey," the lady says to me as she rises from her chair. "If you see anything you like, you just let me know."

I point to a row of tiny knitted animals. "Can I see that elephant?"

She holds up the gray elephant and slides it on her finger. "It's a finger puppet." She bends her knuckle, making the puppet wiggle.

"Oh, my goodness. That is so cute. My nephew and niece would love those. How much?"

"Two for five dollars."

This lady is underselling her skills. "In that case, give me an elephant, the dog, the cat, and the tiger."

The little girl places them in a paper bag as I hand the lady a twenty-dollar bill.

"Keep the change," I say, tucking the bag into my oversized purse.

"Thank you so much," the lady says, pride showing all over her face. "Oh, and for your generosity, this is a little something to support Smithville High School."

She hands me a purple-and-yellow foam finger, and I slip it on my hand and point it toward the little girl. "How did you know I've always wanted one of these?"

"Who doesn't?"

"Good point." Waving to them with the foam finger still on my hand, I set off for booth number twelve, to see if Mitch is pulling my leg about his baking abilities.

CHAPTER TEN
Mitch

Now that Chloe doesn't smell like a stink bomb, I walk back to my booth. Regina and Mrs. Cavanaugh are sitting in chairs behind my table, sharing a laugh. God only knows about what, and I am pretty sure I don't want to know.

Regina holds out her arms. "Give me that sweet girl."

I turn my back on her as I stand next to my table. "Nope. Very few people can resist a baby, so I'm going to use it to win some votes."

Mrs. Cavanaugh looks over her wire-rim glasses. "Like that out-of-towner? Looked like Chloe was working her charm on her."

Heat flames my neck as I focus on the miniature pies sitting on my table. "Chloe is too young to know better."

"Uh-huh," Regina says to Mrs. Cavanaugh. "Chloe could teach her uncle a thing or two."

"What's that supposed to mean?"

Regina points in the distance, where Jackie stands watching people do the two-step on a makeshift dance floor. She sways her hips and claps like she's one of us, a foam finger sticking out of her massive purse. "You two were seriously throwing out some pheromones out there."

"I think what you were seeing was anger coming from me. She assumed since I was holding a baby that it had to be mine. Who does she think she is?"

Regina rolls her eyes. "Get over yourself. It's obvious she was fishing for info about you."

"Not hardly. Besides, that is not the kind of fishing I do."

Regina groans. "Good Lord, Mitch. Take that stick out of your butt and do some fishing of your own."

Mrs. Cavanaugh chuckles as she hands the mayor one of my pies.

To the mayor, I say, "Don't forget to vote for my pie."

He takes it out of the plastic bag and shoves the entire dessert into his piehole. He smacks his lips while he talks. "Tasty. Creamy, and the crust. Mm-mmm."

When the mayor walks away, Regina says to Mrs. Cavanaugh, "Intruder alert."

I swing around, still holding Chloe, to see Jackie heading my way. Her head down, she's scribbling on her scorecard as the foam finger whacks the mayor in the leg. She glances up, then back down. When she looks up again, she sees me glaring at her.

"What?"

"Well, if it isn't the journalist."

She gasps and looks around her. "You really need to move past that. I'm not here to deal with doubters." She narrows her eyes at me. "And furthermore, you shouldn't make me mad since I hold your baking career in my hands."

I peer over to her scorecard to get a gander at how she's been grading the pies. She clamps it close to her chest. "No peeking." She turns her attention to my table. "Hello there, Mrs. Cavanaugh. Nice to see you again."

"Good day, Miss Myers. I hope everyone is being neighborly toward you."

Jackie cuts her eyes toward me. "Not everyone."

Regina smacks the table, making Chloe jump in my arms. "Mitch, do I have to sic my fiancé after you?"

Jackie points a finger from me to Regina with a puzzled expression on her face. "So, you're not..."

"Oh God no," Regina and I say at the same time.

I add, "You sure do want me to have a wife today."

Regina snarls. "Don't mind him. He has no manners. I'm engaged to his brother, Clint."

Jackie raises her eyebrows, and her mouth forms a perfect O. I can't tell if she's relieved or if she doesn't believe Regina. Not that I care either way.

"We'd kill each other if we had to spend any more time together than we do."

Regina rolls her eyes. "That's the gospel truth."

Mrs. Cavanaugh points to the far side of the festival. "Here comes the rest of the young 'uns."

We all turn and see Marlo dragging a twin from each hand as they squirm, trying to get away.

Jackie picks up a pie and inspects it like she's a judge on the British Bake Off. "What's in the filling?"

With a flat grin, I say, "Family secret."

Caleb bumps the table, and if it weren't for Regina's quick reflexes, my pies would have landed in the grass.

"What I mean is, are there any nuts in the filling?"

"No, but—" I get body-slammed by Carson, who crawls up my leg and onto my back, causing me to let out an "oof."

"Unc Mitch, Mama's mad at us for climbing the wall to the dunk tank."

"Why did you do that?"

Caleb, who can't let his twin brother get the upper hand, says, "'Cause she told us not to."

"Dudes, that is not a way to behave. You should listen to your mother."

Marlo rushes up to us, crosses her arms over her chest, and taps her toes. "Boys, that's it. We are going home."

The twins bow their heads in shame. "We're sorry, Mama."

"Too bad. You promised you would be good, and you've been everything but good." Marlo's face goes from angry to concerned. "Are you all right?" she asks Jackie.

I turn my attention toward Jackie, who is pawing at her throat. In less than sixty seconds, her lips change from lusciously plump to looking like she overdid it with the Botox injections. I grab her by the shoulders and ask in my stern EMT voice, "Are you okay?"

She shakes her head as she lets the remainder of the pie fall to the ground. "Nuts. I'm..."

Regina climbs over the table and helps me sit Jackie down on the ground. "Do you have an EpiPen?"

Jackie wheezes and nods at the same time as she reaches for her purse. I snatch it out of her hand and toss items out onto the ground: the foam finger, a wallet, a work ID, a bottle of Advil, and a paper. Finally, tucked all the way at the bottom is an EpiPen that looks like it's as old as me. Quickly, I check the expiration date, and sure enough, it expired three years ago.

"Regina, grab my bag from under the table."

Holding Jackie's hand, I speak in a calm voice. "I want you to focus on me. Try to slow your breathing."

A tear trickles down her cheek, and I swipe it away while Regina unzips my medic bag and fishes out an EpiPen, one that I know hasn't expired. Helping her to a sitting position, I slide up her dress so her thigh is exposed then jab the injection into her leg for a full five seconds before removing it. While I count Jackie's pulse, Regina pulls out my blood pressure cuff and proceeds to pump it up around her arm.

Jackie begins to take deep breaths again, and I let out a sigh of relief. "Regina, can you call 911 so she can be transported to the ER?"

"Not going to a small-town emergency room."

"Yes, you are. It's protocol. I'll ride with you if that makes you feel better."

She snorts. "It makes me feel worse." She hugs her knees and rocks back and forth while I rub her back in hopes she will relax.

"They're on their way." Regina kneels beside Jackie. "You're going to be fine. I'm a nurse, and Mitch is an EMT, so you're in good hands."

Her head snaps toward mine, her jaw slacked. "You're an EMT, and you let me eat something with peanuts."

"It was pecans, and I wouldn't say I let you—"

"I asked you if it had nuts, and you said no. Are *you* nuts?" Her puffy lips muffle her words.

"Of course not." I scan the area and find crumpled in the grass the display that shows my tent number and a nut allergy warning on it. I pick it up and show it to her. "Ma'am, this fell off the table. I would never let you purposely eat something—"

"Ambulance is here." Mrs. Cavanaugh is stuffing Jackie's things back into her purse.

"Great," Jackie says. "This is just great."

Frank and Danny show up, dragging a gurney through the grass. We discuss what happened, and in less than two minutes, they have rechecked her vitals and gingerly placed her on the gurney. Jackie covers her face with her hands as onlookers watch her being whisked away.

While I walk next to them on the way to the ambulance, she waves me off. "Stay here and hand out your precious pies."

I've just about had it with her attitude. I didn't do anything wrong, and I helped her. "You need to get it through your thick skull that I'm going with you. Get over it."

As I slide in next to Danny in the back of the ambulance, Jackie gives me a stare that would put fear into a lesser man. "You have no idea what you just did. You will pay for this."

"Myers, I'm already paying for it. You sound like Elmer Fudd, so stop talking or people will think your hunting waaabbits."

Danny belts out a laugh. If I thought for a second her life was still in danger, I would never joke around like this. But her O2 sats are normal, and maybe a little humor will help her relax.

"Not funny."

"You got that right. I'm a Daffy Duck fan myself," I say with a cheesy smile.

Danny stares from me to Jackie, then back to me. "Is this your new girlfriend?"

"No," Jackie and I yell at the same time.

Danny chuckles and motions for Frank to drive to the hospital. This woman is the bane of my existence, and now, I'll never win the pie contest.

CHAPTER ELEVEN
Jackie

The confined ambulance makes my throat close up worse than the pecans. I've scratched so much, there are probably bloody streaks down to my collar bones. I rise off the gurney, but the ambulance turns a corner, and Mitch grabs my shoulders before I tumble onto the floorboard.

"Hey now, Elmer. We're almost there."

The blaring siren pounds through my head, and I mumble through my swollen lips, "Can you turn off that noise? Oh God, I feel sick."

"Shh." Mitch reaches for my hand. "Frank, she's stable. Can you cut the horn?"

The silence is deafening, but the pounding in my head does subside.

"All vitals are within normal range again."

Mitch pulls off my sandals, and I lurch upward. "What are you doing?"

His mouth twitches as he rests my feet in his lap. "Your feet are as swollen as your lips."

I do my best to suck in my lips, but it's impossible. I've only had one other reaction like this before, and it was so long ago, I almost forgot what it felt like.

The EMT sticks my arm and begins fluids. "You should feel better soon. It's a good thing Mitch was there to save your life."

I laugh, but it makes my stomach churn. "This is all his fault." I wish I could talk normally again, but my puffy lips aren't letting me.

"Myers, you are impossible." He rubs the arches of my feet, and my swollen eyelids close as I let a moan of satisfaction. Mitch has magical hands, and he's actually helping to take my mind off this horrible incident, even if he did cause it.

The ambulance slows to a stop, and the EMT opens the back door. With my purse under his arm, Mitch helps the EMT wheel me inside the hospital.

"I'm fine now."

"It's protocol, so you'll have to bear with the team. Once they clear you, you'll be able to leave and torture some other poor soul." Mitch winks, and I want to scream.

The ER staff wheels me into a bay surrounded by a curtain, and a nurse comes in and introduces herself as Jolene.

"Hey, Mitch. I didn't know you were working today."

"I'm not."

"I wish I wasn't. I always draw the short straw on festival days. Did you know Ursula got admitted?"

HIPAA violation.

"She's claiming she got food poisoning from Jess Boyden's chicken on a stick."

Mitch snorts. "Everyone knows not to eat her cooking."

After she sanitizes her hands, she checks my blood pressure again. From my purse, my phone rings.

"Want me to get that for you?" Mitch asks me.

I nod. He rummages around in my purse, placing some of my items on the bed next to me. "Maybe it's Bugs."

Ha-ha.

The nurse charts my information in the medical record system. "The doctor will be right in." Then she leaves.

He hands me my phone then freezes.

I check my missed calls, and it was just Brett again, so I place my phone on my stomach, facedown.

He cocks his head to the side, then with the smarmiest of smirks, he picks up the finger puppets. "Myers, is this some kind of kinky toy?"

"What? No." I grab for them, but he steps out of my reach. "They're finger puppets for my niece and nephew."

"Suuure they are." He slides on two puppets, one on each index finger. In a silly, high-pitched voice, he asks, "Mr. Dog, do you believe Myers?" He wiggles his finger while he talks. He shakes the dog puppet like he's saying no. "I do not, Mr. Cat. That Myers girl is a perv."

I hold my hand out to him. "All right, give those to me."

He grins and hands them over. Then he looks down at my bed and spies the lanyard attached to my work ID. "What do we have here?" He dangles it from his index finger, just out of my reach. "Jacqueline M. Dalton, JD. Southeast Hospital Association. Is there something you want to tell me, Myers? Or is it Dalton?"

Crapitty crap. "No."

The doctor enters the room, and I say to Mitch before he leaves the bay, "I'll explain later."

He shakes his head as he exits, like I've done something to wrong him. He was the one who let me eat a pie with nuts in it, and I almost died. This is definitely going in my report. He's making my job so much easier, and I haven't even started yet.

LYING BACK ON THE GURNEY, staring up at the ceiling tiles, I eat a cherry Popsicle a like five-year-old kid. The curtain skitters open, and Mitch stands there, wearing a stern expression. I do *not* want to have this conversation with him right now.

I hold out my Popsicle. "Want some?"

He crinkles up his nose and shakes his head. "I might get cooties."

"Ha. I haven't heard that in a while."

"You sound better. Look better too. I mean, you look less... puffy."

"I think that was meant as a compliment, but I actually do feel so much better. That hasn't happened in at least ten years."

He sits on the rolling stool, scoots closer to my bed, then lets out an exasperated sigh. "You want to explain why you're in Smithville?"

"You want to explain why you, as an EMT, would let me eat nuts when I specifically asked if your pie had nuts?"

Mitch clenches his jaw and takes a deep breath. "You asked if there were peanuts in the filling, and there aren't. There are pecans in the crust. Before I could say anything else, I got attacked by my nephews. And they knocked over the sign. I *did* have a notice about using nuts at my table."

"Who in their right mind makes a pie crust out of pecans?"

He freezes, and the muscles in his jaw clench. "I do. My mother did, too, for that matter. Lots of people around here do."

"The apple, or in this case, the nut doesn't fall far from the tree."

Mitch stands so fast, the stool slams into the wall behind him. "Look, I don't know why you're here, but let me say this again slowly so you can get it through your thick skull."

I gasp. *The nerve of him.*

"I. Did. Not. Intentionally let you eat the pie. In fact, you should thank me."

"What?"

"Yeah. Your EpiPen expired three years ago. Why do you even carry that dud around? If it weren't for me, you would be in the morgue right now."

My mouth opens, but no words come out. No one has ever bested me in an argument before. My mother used to say I was born to be a lawyer, but Mitch makes me lose my thoughts.

He stalks toward my bed, and he crosses his arms as he towers over me. "What are you up to?"

I've only been here one day, and I've already messed up. Mitch is going to find out eventually anyway, so I might as well spill. I squeeze my eyes shut and say in rapid fire, "I'm here to find a reason to shut the hospital down."

When I have the nerve to open my eyes, I find he hasn't moved. His expression hasn't changed. He just stares down at me then lets out a nervous chuckle. "You can't be serious."

I point to my purse. "You saw my badge. My middle name is Myers, last name is Dalton, and Smithville Regional is owned by Southeast Hospital Association. It's my job to be here."

"It's... your job to put people out of a job. How very humane of you."

After taking the last bite of my Popsicle, I place the wooden stick on the bedside table and try to sit up. The paper barrier on the hospital gurney crinkles with my every move, and by the way he slaps a hand over his eyes, I may have given him a view of my nether regions. *Darn these hospital gowns.* "I was supposed to come here to see for myself that we could cut this hospital from our budget. It already looks bad on paper."

"I knew it. No one comes to Smithville for an 'article.'" He uses air quotes around his last word.

Before I can stop myself, I say, "Convince me otherwise."

He snaps his head around so fast, I think he's going to get a concussion. "Me?"

"Yeah. I know the stats, and I can walk the halls and see how the hospital operates and possibly catch a few minor infractions... By the way, you and the nurse talking about the lady who got food poisoning? Yeah, HIPAA violation. But maybe I need a perspective from a 'boots on the ground' person to add to my report."

My boss is not going to like this.

He takes a deep breath then chews on the inside of his lip as he paces back and forth in front of me. He rubs his temples and lets out a groan. Mitch rotates his broad shoulders and, with his hands on his hips, mulls over my proposition. "Okay, *Myers.* You've got a deal. You give me a week to show you how much this hospital means to the community, and if you still aren't convinced, you can do what you think you need to do."

Mitch holds out a hand for me to shake, and when I take his hand in mine, I immediately regret the contact. I flick my eyes up to stare into his deep-blue orbs, and I know I need to steer clear of his touch if I'm going to stay professional.

After all, this is just business.

CHAPTER TWELVE
Mitch

Yep. She flashed me. I'm one hundred percent confident the little weasel didn't mean to, but sometimes those hospital gowns allow these things to happen quite easily. At least I had the decency to cover my eyes.

While I check my text messages, Jolene enters the bay again and gives Jackie her discharge instructions and a new EpiPen. "Make sure you keep this with you at all times and don't stab it into your thumb."

"I know." Jackie's snobby reaction is not necessary. With an annoying twang, she adds, "This ain't my first rodeo."

Jolene, who is usually the pissiest of all nurses, blinks back tears. She paints on a false smile and replies, "That's good."

"Hey now. Jolene is just trying to do her job. Don't jump her case when you're the one with the expired pen to begin with. Don't you check it on a regular basis?"

Jackie bites her bottom lip, which is beginning to deflate to a normal shape. "Sorry. I'm just very frustrated right now."

"Get in line." I grin, but it is the complete opposite of what I'm feeling.

Snapping back into nurse mode, Jolene taps the information into the electronic medical record. "Have you heard from Mel?"

"Nope."

Jolene continues to type on the keyboard as she says, "I just thought after she pulled that stunt then skipped the country—"

"Haven't heard from her. Can you wrap this up?" I wish I could transmit my thoughts to Jolene to stop talking in front of the person who will use any excuse to put us all out of a job.

"Yep. Is there someone I can call to drive you home?" she asks Jackie.

Jackie shakes her head. "I'll walk. It can't be that far."

"I'm sorry, ma'am, but hospital policy won't allow that."

Ha! Take that Miss "Looks Bad on Paper."

She tugs on the strings of her gown and lets out a whiny groan. "Can't you make an exception for an out-of-towner? My closest acquaintance is about an hour away."

My eyebrows rise. "You want Jolene to bend the rules?"

She sneers at me. "Of course not."

Jolene clicks a pen. "Would you like me to call him or her?"

"No, you may not call *him*. He's a colleague of mine, and he's the last person I want to know about this. Could you just call me an Uber?"

I flick my eyes to Jolene and say in a flat tone, "Yeah, Jolene. Call her an Uber."

Jolene turns to leave and rolls her eyes so only I can see her. "I'll get right on that... Uber."

Jackie jumps off the bed and gathers up her clothes. "I'm sorry. I didn't mean to come off so rude to her, but there really isn't anyone I can depend on to drive me one single mile. Do you mind turning around? I need to change."

Throwing up my hands in frustration, I say, "Okay, but you'll be waiting here until next Thursday for that Uber. I guess it's your first rodeo needing a ride in the sticks."

She swirls her finger under my nose. "Turn around."

"Fine," I growl. "It's not like I haven't seen everything already."

"You take that back."

I face away from her and stare at the ceiling. "I meant with my job. Sometimes, you gotta rip off clothes, and body parts get exposed. In my line of work, I've seen enough boobs and pubes to last a lifetime."

I hear her grumble under her breath, then in a soft voice, she says, "Could you zip me up? Ugh. I'm puffy everywhere."

"That means I would have to turn around and look at you, two things you said for me not to do."

"You have permission to do both."

I face her as she forces the two sections of her sundress together. My fingers graze hers as I zip it up. Because she's still a little swollen from her reaction, the dress is pretty snug, but she wears it well.

When she's fully zipped up, she sighs. "You're not going to say anything, right? About my J.O.B."

"For now, *Myers,* I'll keep your secret. Or what should I call you now?"

She steps up to me, her face as red as her hair. Her lips are plump, but not puffy anymore, and the splotches across her neck are subsiding. "Myers is fine. I promise I'll be objective and fair. Can you say the same thing?"

I take a step closer, so close, I can see the flecks of gold in her brown eyes. "Absolutely."

Her gaze darts down to my mouth for only a second, but I catch it. My mouth twitches in response. Just as she's about to say another smart-aleck comment, Jolene returns.

I take a quick step backward to get my wits about me. I do not need to notice her pretty eyes and especially not her lips. But more than that, I certainly don't need to give Jolene any ammo to spread through the rumor mill.

"Ma'am, I'm afraid there isn't an Uber within a hundred miles."

A rumble of laughter resonates through the emergency room. "Told ya. Jolene, I'll take her back to the Peach Fuzz Inn."

Jolene flinches, and her nose scrunches up. "Don't use the home-made peach soap. They say it's gentle, but I swear, it burned my cousin's hide off her face. And oh, good gracious, the wedding photos were a disaster."

I grimace. "Thanks for the tip, Jo." I cock my head to the side and focus on Jackie. "Wasn't that quite neighborly of Nurse Jolene to offer that advice when she didn't have to?"

With a flat smile, she replies, "Quite neighborly."

Jolene's eyes brighten. "Are you here visiting family?"

Jackie fidgets with her dress until it's a wrinkled mess. She glances at me, as if I'm going to give her the lie she's looking for. "No, I, uh—"

"She's here on assignment."

Her eyes grow bigger, and her mouth drops open. My guess is she's trying to decide if I'm going to rat her out or keep up the charade a bit longer.

"She's going to write an article about small-town living."

Jolene perks up and squeals. "If you're from *Southern Living*, you have to visit my mama's yard. She has some of the oldest lilies in the region, and they're the prettiest, if I do say so myself. My grandma transplanted them from her nana's yard, and if I'm not mistaken, my great, great—"

"I'll be in touch," Jackie says, halting Jolene's horticultural soliloquy.

"You know where to find me." Jolene waves goodbye as she leaves the emergency bay.

Jackie and I stare at one another for a moment before I break the silence. "I'll get my truck."

"Yee-haw. Wait. You rode in the ambulance with me. How are you going to drive me in your truck?"

I pull out my cell phone. "There's this new-fangled invention down here called a cell phone. I punch in a few numbers and can send a message to someone without even having to talk to them."

With an eye roll, she groans. "Fascinating."

"Regina is dropping off my truck."

"But—"

"The keys are in the glove box. You've seen my sled. No one is going to steal it."

"True."

I clutch my chest with my hands. "Ouch. Most people don't diss Roberta, even in her advanced age, and live to tell about it."

Jackie snickers. "Roberta? I would think you would name it something crankier, like—"

"Like Jackie?"

She holds her fist out for me to bump. "Touché. Let's get out of here. Hospitals give me the creeps."

I must have been an evil monster in a former life, and this is my punishment. My brain still hasn't completely processed the fact that Mel left and I was an idiot for so many years. I don't have the energy to talk to another woman, let alone spend any significant amount of time with her. But now, without thinking things through, she's about to climb into my truck and into my life for the next week, all for the sake of keeping the hospital open. *This is going to be the longest week ever.*

WE RAMBLE DOWN THE street in my truck in silence, then she points to the left. "You need to turn here."

"I'm *from* here. I'm pretty sure I know how to get to the inn. Are you always this bossy?"

Jackie smirks. "I'm usually a bitch."

I guffaw as I turn left onto Pine Avenue. "Let me know if there is an easy button I can push so I can just bypass the bossy in you."

"You're not taking me to Jolene's mother's house, are you? Because I don't know the first thing about flowers."

I pause long enough to make her squirm, then say, "No, but it is the prettiest yard in town."

Her eyes grow wide as she points outside. "Are those chickens?"

"Yep. Wild chickens everywhere."

"I guess it gives a new meaning to why the chicken crossed the road. To get to the Piggly Wiggly."

My lip is going to be ripped to shreds because I'm biting it so much. That was funny, but I'll never let her know that.

With her cell phone, she snaps a picture of the chickens. "No one will ever believe me unless I have photographic evidence. So... Mitch, what's your story?"

"What do you mean?"

She shrugs. "I don't know. I've met your brother. What else is in your backstory?"

"Clint is my younger brother. Silas is the oldest. The two rug rats and the baby girl belong to him."

Jackie lets out a content sigh. "She is so adorable."

"She takes after her uncle."

She leans over and stares at my crotch.

"What are you doing?"

"The baby had a poopy diaper, so I was checking. Like uncle, like niece."

Heat flames my ears as I grip the steering wheel. "All right, Myers. Your turn. Brothers?"

She shakes her head. "Nope. One sister who got her MRS degree from Vanderbilt Law. My father won't let it go."

I nod. "Dads can be that way."

She lands a playful punch to my shoulder.

"Ow."

"You got daddy issues too?"

"Don't we all?"

After a long pause, she says, "That's all I'm getting out of you about family?"

"Yep." There isn't enough gold in Fort Knox to get me to share about my dysfunctional family with her.

She pokes out her bottom lip, and something inside me flutters, which infuriates me. "Pfft. You're no fun. Where did you go to college?"

The flutter is squelched, thank goodness. My knuckles turn white from gripping the steering wheel so hard. "I took a few classes at the community college in Douglas, enough to get my EMT cert, but no, I did not go to college. Neither did my older brother, Silas, and he turned out just fine. And if it weren't for baseball, Clint wouldn't have gone either."

She nods as if she gets my meaning, but I doubt she can ever understand my situation. Being poor is just the tip of the iceberg. "Next topic. Since we're going to spend time together this week, how many girls are going to try to give me food poisoning or slash my tires?"

I whip my head around to see if she's joking. "Why would you ask that?

Turning back to face the road, I feel Jackie staring at me. She spits out a laugh. "I only assume there's a flock of local girls who would not like me hanging out with the Smithville—"

"Hardly." I pull into a parking space in front of the inn. I cut the engine and turn to stare at her. "I'll report back to Jolene that you got to your destination safe and sound. You know, to document accordingly. We wouldn't want to give 'the man' a reason to shut us down."

"Thank you for being my transportation." She touches her lips and adds, "I think they are almost back to normal."

She shouldn't bring attention to her mouth. I give myself a mental slap on the face and say, "Aw, that's too bad. I was enjoying the company of a Looney Tunes character."

Jackie lets out an exasperated groan and unbuckles her seatbelt. "Ha-ha. What's in store for tomorrow? Since it's Sunday, I only have a two o'clock Skype meeting, so other than that, I'm free."

Skype. Zoom. I bet she thinks outside the box and also believes teamwork makes the dream work.

I take a moment to hash over what I can do to convince her the hospital needs to remain open. She's probably already got her mind made up, so this "You've got a week to convince me" crap is more likely just a way for her to play hooky from work. I need to spend seven days with a strong-willed woman as much as a boar hog needs tits, but Regina's words ring in my head. I can't change the data, but maybe I can get Jackie to fall in love with the town.

I grin and say, "Fishin'."

Her eyebrows rise, and by her expression, that was the last thing she expected me to say. "Fishing?"

"Yep. I'll pick you up at six thirty. The fish are hopping this time of year. Oh, and wear old clothes. I'm making a big assumption here, but I'm guessing you didn't think to pack waders." I flash her my killer smile for added effect.

With a cheesy grin, she says, "If I had only known, I would have brought my Prada pair. Super cute and very 'in' these days."

"All righty, Miss Sassy Pants, I'll bring an extra pair. Do you prefer purple or one with sparkles?"

Jackie pantomimes strangling me.

Mission accomplished.

CHAPTER THIRTEEN

Jackie

Penny's giggles don't help the fact that I'm googling "how to fish" because I have never been near a live fish in my life, except when I took my niece to the Georgia Aquarium last year.

"Not funny."

"He must be really cute if you're going fishing instead of sleeping in."

Too cute. After a deep exhale, I say, "No matter how cute he is, I need to do this."

"So he *is* cute."

I know better than to try to sugarcoat the situation for Penny. As my one true confidant at work, she knows my moods better than I do. "Here's the thing. I kind of outed myself by accident to Mitch when my face was all swollen from an anaphylactic reaction. I didn't know—"

"Hold the phone. Back up. Say that again."

"I'm sending you a photo, but you're in the cone of silence."

"Cone of silence. Got it."

I switch to FaceTime, and when she sees the picture of my splotchy face, Penny covers her mouth, but that doesn't stop another round of giggles from erupting.

"Not funny. I mean, who in the world puts nuts in a pie crust?"

"My grandmother used to do that. It's rather tasty."

"So, after he let me eat his pie, I had a raging reaction, then he saved me because my EpiPen wasn't effective. He found my ID. I had to confess my reason for coming to this... peculiar town."

"You like that place already. I can sense it."

I flop back onto my bed and relive yesterday's events. The soft sheets beckon me to lie there for another hour or two. But I have a feeling that if I'm not outside waiting on Mitch, he'll come up and drag me out of the bed. I do not need him anywhere near my bed.

"I do not."

"Denial."

She has no idea what I've seen so far. From nut crust to chickens literally crossing the road, this town is far from sleepy or quaint. "Enough about that. Do you think you can stall the big meeting for a week?"

"Why?" Penny asks, raising her eyebrows.

"I might have agreed to give Mitch one week to convince me that shutting the hospital down is a bad idea."

"Ah. Hence the fishing. I see."

"Well, I don't. What does fishing have to do with the hospital?"

Penny raises a shoulder. "I guess you'll find out soon enough."

A bang to my door scares the crap out of me. "I've got to go."

"Send me a pic."

I disconnect our FaceTime before she gets a chance to say anything else.

After one last look in the mirror, I sling open the door, and as they say down here, *Lord have mercy.* Mitch stands before me in an olive-green T-shirt that stretches tight across his muscles, tan cargo shorts, ratty hiking boots, and of course, an Atlanta Braves baseball cap. And that grin... He lights up the room with those smiley eyes.

"You ready?"

That's a loaded question, one I'm afraid to answer.

Throwing my arms open wide, I ask, "Is this okay? I didn't pack for fishing."

His eyes do a long, slow roam down my body and now I wish I had worn a parka. His gaze drinks me in, and I suddenly feel very undressed, despite my baggy T-shirt and running shorts.

Mitch blinks a few times then clears his throat. Staring at his feet, he mumbles, "You look amazing—I mean, you look fine."

Breaking the spell, I grab my purse and point to the door. "Okay, then. Let's go."

I follow him as he gallops down the stairs and out the front door of the inn. His swagger is mesmerizing, and when he stops on a dime, I run into him. His wall of muscles halts me from face-planting onto the sidewalk. His raised eyebrow is a dead giveaway that he caught me staring at his butt. I push off his taut body and internally kick myself for acting like a stupid teenager.

"Sorry. I was enjoying the scenery. I mean, the flowers."

He plucks a mum from the planter next to the porch and hands it to me.

I take a whiff.

"Sniff away. Maybe you can add it to your article for *Southern Living*. Let's go."

This morning is starting off on the wrong foot.

MITCH HEADS UP A LONG driveway toward a gorgeous log home overlooking a massive lake. A mallard flies by and lands on the other side of the lake to round out the scene.

"Wow," I say, shielding my eyes with my hand. "I don't know what's more spectacular, the house or the lake."

"The house is Gunnar and Andie's. This side of the lake is theirs too."

"I bet sunsets are breathtaking."

"Yeah." He lets out a sigh that almost sounds sad. "It's one of my favorite places."

"To clear your head?"

He nods. "Yep." Mitch parks in the driveway and walks away from the house toward a wooden dock by the lake. "The boat is over there. It's Gunnar's, but he lets me use it whenever I want."

A shaggy dog runs up to me and puts his huge paws on my chest, knocking me down with an "oof." The dog licks my face like I'm covered in peanut butter.

"Griff, give the lady some space." Mitch grabs the dog by the scruff of his neck and forces him off me.

I prop myself up on my elbows and look up at Mitch. "His manners are no better than yours."

"At least I don't bite... much."

He lowers a hand to help me up, but I swat it away. "I can do this myself."

That's me—never asking for help with anything.

He backs away, shaking his head. "If you say so, Elmer."

"Don't start that again." Although the comparison is funny, I won't let him know it. I stand, dust off my backside, and say, "Let's do this."

Mitch stands with one foot inside a small metal boat and one foot on the dock as he holds out a hand to me. "Steady or you'll send me to the bottom of the lake."

As I take his hand, I let out a chuckle. "Don't tempt me."

As I settle into the boat, he unties it from the dock and starts up the engine. He turns his Braves baseball cap backward and revs the engine. I cling to the side as we skim across the lake. My hair whips around my face, and I feel as free as a bird. We haven't made it one hundred feet from the dock, and Mitch's demeanor has already changed from grumpy cat to super chill. It's as if just being out here on the water relaxes him enough to remove the perma-scowl.

He cuts the engine when we reach a shady spot on the other side of the lake. Mitch proceeds to bait my hook with a cricket and hands me the fishing rod. "Do your best not to catch *me*."

That has a double meaning, I'm sure. I let my line drop right next to the boat and sit. "So, what do we—"

"Shh."

"But—"

In a voice barely above a whisper, he shushes me. "Fishing involves a lot of waiting. In silence."

He casts his line out close toward the shore, and slowly reels it in, over and over. Other than the birds chirping, there is no other sound for the next hour as he catches fish after fish, then lets them go. I gape as his forearm muscles flex each time he tosses his line out and slowly reels it back in. The rhythm is mesmerizing.

A tug on my line wakes me up from gaping at his tense forearms. After another tug, I drop the pole—into the lake.

Mitch turns around and yells, "Why did you do that?"

Throwing my hands up like I'm under arrest, I squeak out, "I don't know."

He lurches toward me, grabbing for the pole. I do my best to get out of his way, but my movements are too brisk and the boat rocks. My foot slips out from under me, kicking Mitch in the shins. His hands flail in the air, and before I can lean forward to grasp his hand, he flops backward into the lake with a large splash. To keep from going in right on top of him, I grab the side of the boat and ride out the rocking.

Mitch surfaces and whips the water off his face. Holding on to the side of the boat, he stares up at me. "You did that on purpose, didn't you?"

"I most certainly did not," I say through a fit of giggles.

He splashes water on me, and I squeal. "I don't believe you, but if you don't want to capsize this boat, move all the way to the other end while I hoist myself up."

"Yes, sir."

I crawl to the far end and hold on for dear life while he shimmies up onto the boat. He drags his wet T-shirt off his body, and I almost fall

backward into the lake watching him wring it out. *Damn, he is ripped.*
To keep myself from drooling, I stare out at the water and do my best
to pretend I'm astutely interested in freshwater wildlife. With a *fwop*,
his wet T-shirt lands on my face.

Like I'm being stung by a thousand wasps, I fight to remove it without going overboard.

"That's for making me fall out of the boat."

I lean over and grab his baseball cap, which is bobbing in the water.
"I think I found a souvenir."

"Give it."

"Nope." I slide it onto my head backward, like he was wearing it. "I
fit right in, don't you think?"

Cranking the boat engine, he huffs. "That will *never* happen."

Once we're back to the dock and he safely assists me onto dry land,
I hand him his T-shirt. He slaps it over his shoulder, slinging water
along with it. "You're lucky I have a smidgen of manners, because if I
was all by my lonesome and that had happened, I would have stripped
buck naked."

I immediately pivot so he can't see my blood-red face as I imagine
him with no clothes on. A shirtless Mitch has my ovaries pinging
around in my abdomen. If he was completely naked, I don't think I
could keep my brain working long enough to stop my hormones from
taking over, allowing me to climb him like a tree.

"I appreciate that," I say as I stand on the deck. "Thank you, by the
way."

"For what?"

As I stare out over the water, a hawk swoops down to grab a snack
from the lake. "For bringing me here. It's so calm and relaxing, I can actually breathe out here."

He turns to watch what has caught my attention. "Even in a small
town, sometimes I feel too overwhelmed with people. It's nice to come
here to think and not have to talk."

"So, what does this have to do with saving the hospital?"

He dips his head low as he ties the boat to the dock. When he stands back up, he grins. "Nothing. I just wanted to go fishing."

"Are you serious?"

"Look at it this way. You can use it as research for your article in *Field and Stream*."

Ugh. He is so annoying.

But that deep husky chuckle as he walks back to his truck, baring way too much skin, is going to be the death of me.

CHAPTER FOURTEEN
Mitch

With Caleb hanging from my neck and Carson clinging to my leg, I do my best to maneuver through my brother's house without causing bodily harm. I love my nephews, but they are a handful on a good day. I don't think the sugar has worn off from the festival, because they are all wilder than usual.

Marlo reads her phone, and her eyebrow quirks up. "Somebody in this family made Biddy's Blog this week."

Trying to pry Carson off my leg, I say, "What did Clint do this time?"

She clears her throat and reads, "If one out-of-towner isn't enough, Smithville has been blessed with a second one, and she's quite nuts for one stud of an EMT."

I feel my body shrink in size as I tickle Carson in an attempt to be nonchalant.

"A fly on the wall-nut told me after a severe nut allergy, the Smithville Stud jumped into the fray and saved this fierce redhead before she cash-ewed in her chips."

Marlo grimaces. "Their puns are getting worse."

Finally free of my nephews, I lean over Marlo to read the rest. "This is totally ridiculous."

Marlo looks back at me and rolls her eyes before she reads on. "While we searched the inter-nut, we can-nut find where this little bomb-shell is from or why she's pining for our Stud."

Of course, they couldn't find her on the internet. Jackie was smart enough not to use her last name. Kudos to her for besting the Jackson sisters.

I point to her phone. "That is not true, the pining part, I mean."

"Hmm. Let me finish. Rumor has it, the two coconuts spent time on the lake today. We must say our local Stud still looks mighty fine without a shirt. We'd eat him up, nuts and all."

My mouth drops open, and I dart my attention to my nephews, who are listening to every word.

"What nuts do you have, Unc Clint?"

Marlo bites her lip and turns her back on her children, leaving me to fend for myself as a giggle escapes her lips.

"I don't have any nuts. I did make a pie with pecan flour crust. She ate a bite, and it made her sick."

Caleb cocks his head to the side, and his little jaw drops. "I can't believe she didn't like your nut dust pie. That's mm-mm good." He rubs his belly for emphasis.

"Thank you, little buddy."

Marlo composes herself enough to take control of the conversation again. "Enough about Mitch's nuts. Let's get ready for dinner."

The front door bursts wide open, and Regina and Clint enter, which causes another round of hyperactivity from the twins. Marlo throws her hands up in surrender. It's one thing to hang all over me, but the twins love Clint, especially since he towers over them. I'm a stump compared to him.

With an evil twinkle in his eye, Clint pops me on the shoulder. "Hey, nutty buddy."

I collapse into the nearest chair and let out a groan.

Regina sits next to me and pinches my cheek. "I'm just glad you're putting yourself out there again. You need to date. This is a good thing. Don't let the Jackson sisters' blog deter this."

Backing away from her, I put my hands up in defense. "Whoa. No-body said anything about dating anyone. She's here for a week, and I was being... neighborly."

They can't know about the little deal I made with Jackie. Plus, I'm not. Dating. Anyone.

"Do neighbors just casually fall into the lake and, by chance, take their clothes off in front of each other?"

Marlo gasps and does her best to cover her boys' ears, but they wriggle free. "We like skinny-dipping," Caleb said. "Is that what you did?"

"No! Not even close. I got off balance and fell out of the boat. When I got back in, I took my shirt off so it could dry faster. End of story."

Did it get hot in here all of a sudden?

Regina's smirk tells me she doesn't believe any of it. "How long have I known you?"

I shrug. "I don't know. Most of my life, I'm guessing."

She nods. "And all this time, how many times have you 'gotten off balance' in the boat and fallen in the lake?"

I swat at her air quotes.

Clint doesn't help me any. He just nods in agreement with his fiancée.

Scratching my head, I delay as long as I can while I search for a reply. There really isn't a good one. I didn't fall into the lake on purpose so I could take off my shirt. If I wanted to impress her, I could have just taken off my shirt. Somehow, I don't think a big-shot corporate lawyer would give two flying flips about what my body looks like. I don't have the proper diplomas hanging on my wall—not that I care anyway.

"It's really—"

I'm interrupted by Silas coming home, and for the third time, the twins go into spaz mode, making their mother sigh with defeat.

"Hey, little brother," he says, "I heard you went for a swim today."

Clint holds out his fist for our older brother to bump. I want to punch both of them in the throats.

I'll never admit it to them, but something about her gets under my skin, and I wonder if she feels it too. Her playful banter along with her ability to give as much as she takes is appealing, and that really terrifies me.

CHAPTER FIFTEEN
Jackie

The flowery wallpaper in my bedroom will not do for a Skype meeting background. And if I sit at my desk, right behind me is a picture of a huge bowl of peaches. I'm at the perfect height for it to look like I'm wearing the bowl as a headdress. With no other viable option, I choose a plain blue background. I wanted to use the one with Elmer Fudd, Daffy Duck, and Bugs, but the last thing I need is to be considered unprofessional.

After my time with Mitch at the lake, I still have a faint fishy smell to my hands, even though I scrubbed my body raw. And I know it doesn't really matter, but I slathered on a ton of makeup to hide the fact that I still have a few hives left from my reaction to Mitch's nuts.

Mitch's nuts. That sounds so much worse than it is. It's his pie's nuts, but now, my mind slides into more vulgar thoughts than it should, especially when I can still visualize every ripped muscle in his chest and back. I do not, for the life of me, understand why he's still single. Maybe he eats those wild chickens raw or something like that, because in the few days I've known him, he seems pretty normal.

Who am I kidding? So far, there is *nothing* normal about Mitchell Sorrow.

Brett's ugly mug pops up on my screen, and it's just the two of us staring at each other. He is shirtless, and his body is the antithesis of Mitch's. He needs to either put on a shirt or hit the gym more often. That spare tire around his middle is not sexy. He still lives like he's in college, and being in a college town for a few days is only amplifying that attitude.

85

"Hey there, compadre."

"Your man boobs don't scream 'promotion' to me."

"Oh, I'm always professional. But you? Not so much. Like the time three years ago when we were at that corporate retreat, and you had a few too many drinks and—"

"Can you just drop that? You know as well as I do that your friend pursued me like a dog in heat." I do a full-body shiver, remembering that weekend when I thought Franklin was on the up and up. Not at all. He was all over me and made me think he was divorced. I'll never forgive myself for falling for his lines. He's smarmy at best, and even if he was available, he certainly isn't my type. I don't even know what my type is anymore, but any associate of Brett's certainly isn't it.

Thinking about "my type" causes Mitch's bare chest to pop into my mind again, and I let Brett's pudgy body fade into the background.

"Why don't you go hit on some college girls?"

"Already did. Leah and Kat will be here in about an hour to start the fun."

"You better hurry because they may have curfews."

"Jealous much?"

I roll my eyes. "Ha. Not in the slightest."

"I bet there isn't one decent, educated guy in that town you're in."

"You might be surprised. My sweet little town is adorable, and the people I've met are... charming."

Brett's eyes squint almost shut. "You met someone, didn't you?"

I truly hate him. "Of course not."

He strokes his chin and smirks. "Keep it up, Dalton. You might fall in love with a hick and never want to move back to Atlanta. I'd hate to win the promotion on a default. Where's the fun in that?"

Sitting taller, I say, "That promotion is mine. Get used to it. And if you aren't nice to me, you can kiss my proofing skills goodbye."

Two more boxes show up on the screen as Matthew and Penny log on to the meeting. Brett slips into a sports coat as Penny and I wave at each other. I notice her little violin sitting on her bed next to her, and it warms my heart that she really likes my gift.

Brett leans close to his screen so it's just his eyes showing, grossing me out. "What's with the makeup job? Going out tonight? A hoedown, perhaps?"

"What's this about a hoedown?" Matthew asks.

"Nothing," I say with a screech. "Brett is just being his usual bratty self."

"Let's make this brief. Brett, are you ready for tomorrow?"

Brett puffs out his chest and puts on his business persona. "Yes, sir. My meeting is set for nine o'clock tomorrow morning, then I plan to work my way through important areas of the hospital. After that, I plan to review the data, complaints filed, yada, yada, yada."

Matthew nods. "After your meeting, don't be too obvious. You're there under the guise of a journalist, not an attorney. We want to see how the hospital runs when no one is watching. So be a fly on the wall."

Brett couldn't be a fly on the wall if his life depended on it. He loves attention and does not blend well.

"Jackie, what about you?"

"Sir, I'm already one step ahead of Brett." I peek over to catch Brett flinch. "I attended a town festival yesterday and witnessed how first responders handle an emergency situation."

Brett scowls. "And..."

"There were some issues that I'll add to my report, but I plan to make the emergency department a priority for my visit tomorrow." Brett and Matthew don't have to know that I've already had that visit, and they certainly don't have to know I was the patient. Not everything has to be included in the report, especially when it comes to patient confidentiality.

Penny gives me a thumbs-up.

"Very good, Jackie," Matthew says. "You see, Brett? This is how it's done. She got in the trenches with the community and discovered some valuable information."

Brett chews on the side of his jaw, his tell-tale sign he's fuming. If this meeting goes on any longer, steam will be coming out of his ears. I give both of them a pleasant smile, and I know Brett will be calling me as soon as the meeting is over. He's nothing if not predictable.

"Okay, I'll leave you two to work, and I'll see you back in the office on Thursday."

The deal with Mitch was for a week, and I'm not a deal breaker. "Sir, do you mind if we postpone the meeting until next Monday?"

"Three days should suffice. We aren't talking about major institutions."

Brett grins. "Yeah, Thursday works for me. I'm already going to need a juice cleanse after spending a few days here. It's grease and sugar everywhere."

"With all due respect, Brett, I like to do a thorough investigation. You may feel like a superficial review is enough, but I want to be extremely detailed in my evaluation. I don't do things halfway."

"Brett, if you want to wrap up by Thursday, that's fine. Jackie, I'm perfectly happy with you taking a little longer, since this is your first attempt at an onsite analysis. Meeting will be rescheduled for Monday at ten o'clock. Penny, can you make sure to update my calendar?"

"Sure thing."

Penny nods. "Call me later," she says before vanishing from the screen. We log off, and before I can count to five, my phone rings. Brett.

"What do you want?"

"You're up to something. I can feel it."

I roll my eyes, even though I know he can't see it. "That feeling is probably a hangover. I'm just doing my job."

"I don't believe you."

With a chuckle, I scratch my neck. "I don't care if you believe me. That's nothing new. You do you, okay? And leave me to do my job."

"Whatever, Dalton."

He disconnects, and I growl. I don't know why I let him get to me. He's like a fifth-grade bully who never grew up. If he ever finds out about what happened at the festival—and especially the arrangement I made with Mitch—I'll never hear the end of it. In fact, it might endanger my job *and* my chances of a promotion. I need to tread lightly with Mitch if I'm going to be objective about my mission.

Like my sister said, eye on the prize.

CHAPTER SIXTEEN
Mitch

Frankie and I ride through town in our ambulance as we gulp down coffee, doing our best to wake up. Mondays are usually quiet, thank goodness. It's the Friday the thirteenths that I dread having to work.

My head is still spinning from the blog and the razzing I got from my family. Clint sent me five different GIFs yesterday about nuts. Regina was even worse. Her messages included hearts and kissy faces. Marlo's messages were all smiley faces. My family loves to meddle so much, I'm thinking about exchanging them, but I doubt trading them in for another family would be any better.

"I know you want to say something, Frankie, so spill."

He snickers. "Nothing."

"I didn't take you to be a fan of the blog."

He shrugs as he turns a corner. "What other entertainment do we have around here?"

"Look, you were there. It was no big deal. She had a reaction to a pie I made."

He pulls into the hospital parking lot and cuts the engine. "That was bad luck, I'll give you that, but what about the part that you two went fishing? Is she someone you met in Douglas?"

"No. She's here for..." I stop to think about why she's here. I can't tell him we all might be out of a job because of her. "She's here for work. That's all I know. I thought I'd be friendly, and since I almost killed her, it was the least I could do. Right?"

Lame.

"Suuure. You forget we've been trapped in the wagon together for a lot of years. I know you like yesterday's news. You've never been 'friendly' before. You've been stuck in this pathetic puppy-love stage for far too long."

"Thanks, bro. How do you really feel?"

Frankie chuckles. "I'm serious, man. I like seeing you... friendly. It's a good look on you."

I slam the ambulance door a little too hard and do my best to ignore his comments. The truth is, I don't know why I asked her to go fishing yesterday. My original intention was for her to like the town, but I guess a part of me wanted her to like me, too, if for no other reason than to see if I had anything left after Mel squashed my heart like a bug.

Regina greets me at the nurses' station. Biting her lip, she buries her head in the chart she's reviewing.

I stare at the ceiling and let out a groan. "Come on, just get it out of your system. Say what's on your mind."

She peeks over the chart and gasps. "Me? What do I want to say?"

Frankie slinks down the hallway toward the break room.

Smart man. "You want to know why I took her fishing? Well, guess what? So do I." I scrub my face with my hands. "I'm so confused."

Regina blinks and puts down the chart. "Mitch, I get it that you've had it difficult ever since the 'doctor that shall be unnamed' left town, so I think it's good that you're dating again."

I run a hand through my hair and, with clenched teeth, say, "I am not dating her."

"You could."

"No, I couldn't. You don't know anything about her." And the little I know about her screams, "Stay away!"

Regina cocks her head to the side. "I don't have to know anything about her. I know you, and it's rare that you put yourself out there. I think it's good."

If she only knew... "You know as well as I do how difficult it is to find something to do around here. We're so hard up, we think moon bathing is fun."

She stands and puts a hand on each of my shoulders. "That's a fantastic idea. Full moon is Wednesday night. You should bring her. It'll be fun."

"No, it won't."

Regina crosses her arms over her chest and huffs. "Why do you think that?"

"Jackie won't want to go."

Behind me, a sexy voice says, "You won't know until you ask me."

I swing around to see Jackie standing there, dressed in a dark-blue business jacket and skirt, carrying a laptop bag. Her auburn hair is up in a professional bun with just a few strands framing her face, and she looks good enough to eat.

"Uh..." My mouth opens and closes, but I can't form any other words.

Regina nudges me toward Jackie. "He hasn't had his second cup of coffee yet."

The radio on my waistband screeches to life, saving me from this rather embarrassing situation. Frankie emerges from the breakroom and points to the door. "Sorrow, we got a call."

Jackie's eyes light up. "Can I ride along?"

"No."

Regina cocks her head to the side. "Why would you want to ride along?"

Jackie's eyes meet mine as she says, "I'm writing an article about small-town living. I'm fascinated by it all."

Regina's eyes brighten. "Are you with *Taste Magazine*? Because if so, you could include Mitch's pie recipe in the article."

Jackie chuckles. "I'll think about it."

Regina glances down the hallway. "If you get in trouble with Dr. Keller, it's not my head that will roll."

"Oh, it will be all right," Jackie says then snaps her mouth shut.

She almost let it slip, so I turn Jackie around and say, "I'll take full responsibility and make sure nothing confidential goes into her... story."

Frankie waves a hand in front of my face. "Dude, we have got to go."

I motion with my head for Jackie to follow us, and I'm already regretting it. She's going to jot down even the least little inaccuracy, which will spell doom for us all.

FRANKIE DRIVES BACK toward the hospital while I tend to a cantankerous Stanley. Jackie sits in the passenger seat, scribbling in a notebook. During the ride to the incident, she asked us a dozen questions about our normal procedures. While I knew her reasons for asking, Frankie really did think she was a journalist, so he boosted his position as much as possible. There were a few times I winced because he was dangerously close to saying something that could jeopardize our careers. But at least she stayed clear of the scene so we could do our job and even kept quiet while on the short ride back toward the hospital with Stanley strapped to the gurney.

I radio into the hospital, "Male, mid-thirties—"

Stanley yells, "I'm not mid-thirties, and you know it."

I peek over to see Jackie fighting off a smile.

"Became dizzy at the packing plant and fell. No visible head trauma. Reports he fell on his... posterior."

Over the radio, Dr. Keller asks, "Vitals?"

"BP: eighty over sixty. Pulse one-twenty and thready. Respirations: twenty-eight and shallow. Temp: ninety-two point six. Skin clammy."

"Ten-four."

"ETA five minutes. Doctor?"

"Yes?"

"Verifying you understood the pulse pressure?"

"Affirmative."

Stanley better not have a heart attack. It's a good thing Jolene isn't working today, because she would cause a scene when we get to the hospital.

After I take his blood pressure again, I pat his arm. "How ya doing, buddy?"

"Fine as frog's hair."

From the driver's seat, Frankie yells, "You hang in there. We're going to take good care of you."

"Almost there. Just relax and enjoy the ride."

Stanley turns his head to look at Jackie and gives her a toothy grin. "Hey there."

"Hi. I hope you don't mind me being here. I'm... doing an article about Smithville."

Her lie seems to get easier to tell every time she spews it.

Stanley grins, and although he's winded, he has enough energy to carry on a conversation. "Are you with *Motor Trend*?"

"Uh... no."

"My daddy has a 1947 REO Speed Wagon that's a looker. You gotta add it to your article."

I glance over at Jackie. "Not the band, but it is a sweet sled."

"I'll remember that."

Stanley puffs out a few breaths before he's able to speak. "You'll like it here. Might not ever want to leave."

I seriously doubt that. She's probably counting the hours before this assignment is over.

"Stan, relax. Dr. Keller will take good care of you."

"I want Melly to doctor me."

With a furrowed brow, I reply, "She's gone. Dr. Keller will be just as good."

I flick my eyes toward Jackie, and she jerks hers toward her notebook. The last thing I want to do is talk about *her* in front of Myers.

"Hey, buddy. Do you want your picture made for her article?"

She sneers, but he brightens up.

"Heck yeah."

I motion for her to hand over her phone, which she does. After a few snaps, I give it back to her. "An article isn't any good without images."

Jackie mumbles to herself as she stuffs her phone back into her pocket.

"We're here. Sit tight."

Frankie and I wheel in Stanley as Jackie race-walks behind us, struggling to keep up. God love him, but Stanley's not the healthiest person on the planet. He's sweating profusely, and if we don't do something soon, he might go into cardiac arrest.

"Hey there, Stanley," Regina says as she slides her fingers around his wrist while walking beside him, counting his pulse as we head toward bay one. "You trying to brighten up my day?"

He chuckles as he pants. "Yeah." *Pant. Pant.* "Guess so."

I pat his arm. "Think of happy thoughts, like what Jolene's got cooking for you."

Frankie locks the gurney into place inside the bay and hands me his meticulous notes.

Stanley rests his head back on the gurney. "I feel sick."

I reach for the emesis basin with no time to spare before Stanley spews the contents of his lunch everywhere. It splatters onto my shirt and pants. Jackie scoots backward just in time to miss getting puked on. Her hand covers her mouth.

"Feel better, buddy?" I ask.

"Yeah." Stanley rests his head back and squeezes his eyes shut.

Dr. Keller and Mara Lee, another nurse, enter, and they douse their hands in sanitizer and don gloves.

Keller barks out orders. "Regina, get an IV started with D5. Mitch, start a tracing."

"Yes, sir."

Dr. Keller points to Frankie. "I need you to call Dr. Lloyd, the hospitalist on duty, and tell him we might have an admission."

Frankie nods.

Stanley grabs my hand. "Don't. Want."

"Don't care." Dr. Keller is not fazed by Stanley's stubbornness. Turning to Frankie, who types the details of the encounter into our computer system, he adds, "See what Mr. Culpepper's blood type is in the medical record system and check for allergies."

"It's O positive," I say. It's odd, but part of my job is knowing certain details of the residents.

"ECG is hooked up," I say as he reads from the strip of paper being printed out of the machine. I point to the tracing and whisper, "No P waves."

"Okay, team. Prepare for cardioversion. Mara Lee, get the cart."

Regina lowers the head of the bed until Stanley lies flat.

"What's... happening?" he asks through shallow breaths.

I place a hand on Stanley's arm. "Stanley, this is going to sound worse than it is, but your heart is not beating right, so the doctor needs to shock it to get it back into rhythm."

He sits up on his elbows. "You're going to *what*?"

"It's okay, Stan," I say as Regina makes a few quick swipes across Stanley's chest with a razor to give the doctor a smooth surface to place the sticky patches. "Dr. Keller knows what he's doing."

"Wanna switch places?"

I let out a deep, rumbly chuckle. "Another day. Today is your day to get all this great attention."

Jackie, her face as white as a sheet, shrinks into the corner of the room, and I appreciate that she doesn't get in the way.

While Frankie placates Stanley, Dr. Keller orders Regina to administer propofol, 2.5 mgs per kg.

"Yes, Doctor."

With the skill of a seasoned ER nurse, Regina starts Stanley's IV and begins the injection while I read another tracing. Frankie hands Dr. Keller the patches and turns on the mechanism.

"Fifty joules please."

Frankie replies, "Fifty joules."

Stanley's eyes become heavy. Propofol is some serious stuff, but it does relax him enough for us to do our job. I place the sticky pads on Stanley's chest.

"Everyone clear," Dr. Keller barks out to make sure all in the room know he means business.

Jackie bumps up against the back wall.

We all take a step backward and hold our hands up in the air as an easy way for Dr. Keller to see no one is touching Stanley. He pushes the button, and Stanley's body does a little jump. My eyes train on the ECG machine in hopes of seeing a normal sinus rhythm.

Dr. Keller shakes his head. "Again. Clear."

When he pushes the button this time, the anticipated QRS tracing shows up, and it's only then that everyone in the room can breathe normally again. Frankie takes Stanley's blood pressure, and while we wait for the results, Regina says, "BP is one-forty over ninety-two."

"Not great, but probably a normal reading for him. Whatever it is, that is a task for another day. His tracing looks normal now, thank goodness."

Dr. Keller glances over at me, and I say, "Nice job."

As he peels off his gloves, he replies over his shoulder, "The entire team did a great job. Frankie, monitor his vitals. Mara Lee, call admissions to see if they have a bed ready. Regina, draw cardiac enzymes. Keep monitoring him, and let me know if he does anything funny."

Before he leaves, Dr. Keller points to Jackie, "And would someone please tell me who this person is and why she's in my ER?"

Jackie throws her shoulders back and sticks out her hand. "I'm Jackie Myers from the *Atlanta Post*, doing an article on Smithville. I hope I didn't get in your way. You did an amazing job back there."

He ignores her outstretched hand. "Harrumph. I'm an ER doctor. That's what I do. If you put any names or any other private information in your article, I will have you fired. Do you understand?"

I do a virtual fist bump with him. *Two points for Dr. Keller.*

She bobs her head up and down. "Of course."

I follow her out of the emergency bay and let out a low whistle. "That was close."

Jackie turns around, her eyes bigger than ever. "That was intense."

With a shrug, I let her compliment roll over me. "Just another day in paradise."

She waves as she starts to walk away, but I touch her arm. "Wait."

Jackie freezes, stares down at my hand wrapped around her bicep, then looks up at me. I'm a big puddle of a human being.

"Would you..." I can't believe I'm going to do this. It will only make things worse for the gossips in this town, but I can't help myself.

"Yes, Mitch?"

After an internal fight with myself, I work up the courage to ask, "Would you like to come to dinner at my brother's house tomorrow night?"

Her eyes brighten. "Really? That's so sweet."

My heart rate is at least one hundred twenty beats per minute, like it's the first time I've ever asked a girl out. When I realize I still have contact with her arm, I jerk my hand away.

"Why?"

"Because you will get tired of the two restaurants in this town, and Marlo is a great cook. Way better than what the Peach Fuzz Inn has to offer. Plus, Marlo's been on my case about it." In a falsetto voice, I add, "Mitch, where are your manners?"

That's totally a lie, but given enough time, Marlo would have started in on me. I just beat her to the punch.

Jackie giggles then works her teeth over her bottom lip, and for a moment, I think she's going to reject my offer. Then she smiles the most beautiful grin I have ever seen. The expression lights up her face. "I would love to."

Mitch, what are you doing to yourself?

CHAPTER SEVENTEEN
Jackie

I cannot believe I said yes to Mitch's offer. He's the most infuriating man on the planet, but he's also very charming and I can't get him out of my head.

I've been trying to tamp down my school-girl crush, but it's very difficult. It's only been four days since we had our first encounter at the gas station, and I'm already feeling a strong pull toward him. So when he asked me to dinner, my heart almost exploded in my chest, it was beating so strongly. Perhaps he feels the connection too. *Or maybe he's just placating his sister-in-law because he's a nice guy, like putting that silly bumper sticker on his truck.*

Without thinking, I call my sister. She'll be able to give me advice.

On the first ring, Gretta answers. "How's it going slumming?"

"This is actually a very adorable community."

She snorts. "I'm kidding. You know that, right? Just don't get schnuckered into their ways. It's a trap to keep you from doing what needs to be done."

I let out a defeated sigh. "I know."

"Sis, what's up?"

I want to reboot my thoughts because it's a bad idea to ask her for advice, especially about men.

"He just asked—"

I squeeze my eyes shut and pray she didn't catch that, but the odds are not in my favor.

Gretta sucks in a deep breath. "Oh. My. God. Are you going on a date?

"It's not a date. Mitch is an EMT, and he's been very helpful."

"You go from Franklin, who is on his way to—"

"I never dated that slimeball. I don't ever want to date anyone like him."

"He has the same goals as you."

Doubtful. "Franklin is a worm. You met him at that one party, and you can't stop trying to pair us off. It's gross."

"He's better than Brett."

My head is about to explode. "Blech."

"You know how these things work. This assignment is just a way for corporate to say a female had the opportunity for the promotion, but the man was a better choice. It will never change."

As much as I want to argue with her, I've had the same thought at least a dozen times. It's difficult and exhausting trying to play the good-ole-boy game.

When I sniffle, Gretta lets out a string of toddler-approved curse words. It's hard to take her seriously when she uses "shooey" and "son of a biscuit eater." "I didn't mean to offend you. You're very good at your job. But women have to fight doubly hard for the same reward. And heaven forbid if we want a career *and* a family."

"It's okay. But you're right."

"Next topic. Tell me more about this Mitch guy."

The stress washes off my shoulders when Mitch's face appears in my mind. Even during our bickering sessions, he's off-the-charts sexy.

"He's different from any other guy I've ever known. And I don't mean because of where he grew up or his level of education. He's very kind... except to me." I chuckle. "I think I push his buttons."

"Yum."

"I get the sense he had a difficult upbringing, but he doesn't use that as a crutch to be a horrible person." In a dreamy voice, I add, "He's just the most interesting person I've ever met."

After a long beat, Gretta finally finds her voice again. "Wow."

"Yeah. He has this immense amount of love for those closest to him, and to me, he's so rich even though he probably doesn't have two pennies to rub together. My bank account is bursting at the seams, but I have no one to share it with. Dollar bills don't keep me warm at night or comfort me when I'm hurting. His wealth cannot be measured by the Dow."

"That's deep, sis."

I shake my head to get my thoughts back on track. "I don't know what came over me."

"Oh, sweetie, he sounds dreamy, but you're too trusting. I don't want you to lose sight of the prize."

"I know. I'll talk to you later."

Tears prick my eyes as I disconnect the call with my sister. "That went over like a lead balloon."

While I write my preliminary report, I pull up the most current statistics for Smithville Regional. There's been an uptake in unpaid health care bills that don't appear to have been transferred to a collection agency. Their bed utility rate is awful, and the net patient revenue has been declining for four years. On paper, this hospital is in really bad shape. For the specialties they offer—there aren't many—they fall into the seventy-fifth percentile for quality of care. They are a hot mess, and my in-person observations will just tip it over into the failing category with no arguments from headquarters.

Drumming my fingers on the desk in my room, I question if it's a good idea to make personal visits. It would be so much easier to analyze the metrics and make a broad-stroke decision. I doubt Brett is struggling with the numbers versus his city's impact—he doesn't have a heart.

A Skype meeting request pops up on my laptop screen, and my heart skips a beat. Thinking I might have forgotten something important, I click on the request, and Brett's ugly mug fills my screen.

"Hey, Jackie. What's up?" His face scrunches up into a prune. "What is all that peach stuff behind you?"

Gesturing with my hand like I'm on *The Price is Right*, I say, "Well, this is the Peach State. Don't you have anything better to do on a Monday night than torture me?"

"I thought we could order in and talk about our hospitals virtually."

My eyes narrow. "You haven't even started on your report, have you?"

He chuckles and scratches his neck. "Chill, Jackie. You need to have a little fun while you're away from the office."

Ignoring his comment, I ask, "What percentage of your staff live out of town?"

"I have no clue."

Shocker. "In Smithville, ninety-five percent of staff, including physicians and administration, live in this county. That's significant."

"Why?"

I stare at his face on the screen. How he cannot get it is beyond me, so I'm not going to explain it to him. "Never mind. I have a big day tomorrow, so I'd like to go to bed early."

"Ugh. You're such a buzzkill."

"Please say goodbye. I'll see you next week."

A knock on my door startles me.

Brett raises an eyebrow. "Expecting someone?"

"No. Goodbye."

"Wait. I have some info from Penny."

I groan. "I'll be right back. Not a peep."

"Sure. Whatever."

I fling open the door to find Mitch standing in the hallway, looking scrumptious.

"Hey. What are you doing here?"

From my laptop, Brett grins. "Honey, who is it?"

If I could, I would reach through my laptop to slap him right now and gladly get arrested for it. Staring at the laptop, I yell, "Shut up."

With his eyes trained on Brett's face on my laptop, Mitch says, "I was making sure you weren't bored, but it looks like that is not an issue."

"No, it's not what you think."

Mitch shakes his head and walks backward. "You don't have to answer to me. I'll pick you up at five o'clock tomorrow for dinner. That is, if you still want to go."

"Go where?" Brett says. "I want to go."

I slam the laptop closed and hope I lose the connection.

My mouth drops open, but no words come out.

The side of Mitch's mouth twitches. In a sing-song voice, he says, "Someone's got a boyfriend." He shakes his head as he turns to leave, not waiting for me to reply. "I better go. See ya."

I hear him trot down the steps, slam his truck door, and peel out of the parking lot. With the wrath of Darth Vader, I open up my laptop again to see Brett's face is still there. "Why did you do that?"

He holds out his hands in defense. "I was just kidding, but that guy has the hots for you."

"He does not."

Brett gives me a knowing look. "Jackie, I know guys, and he was acting all cool-like, but internally, he was furious that you were video chatting with another guy. In his mind, he's thinking the next step would be virtual sex."

"Ew."

"Truth hurts."

I fling my arms in the air. "First of all, Mitch does *not* have 'the hots' for me." I use air quotes to emphasize his choice of words. "And secondly, if he did, you squelched that."

"You. Are. Welcome."

I let out an exasperated groan. "Goodnight, Brett."

"One more thing."

"What?"

"Penny wanted me to tell you the violin was a hit. Not sure what that's supposed to mean, but I promised I would relay that bit of info if I talked to you first."

A grin slides across my face. "Awesome!"

"Later, Jack." He signs off, and I flop back on my bed.

There is no way Mitch is into me. But even the small chance that he is causes an unfamiliar tingle to spread through my body.

CHAPTER EIGHTEEN
Mitch

I need to check my reflection in the mirror, because I'm pretty sure "idiot" is tattooed across my forehead. Of course she has a boyfriend. No woman that gorgeous, smart, and ambitious would be single. I tried to make light of the situation to save face, but I'm not sure my performance was believable.

I really assumed her type would be less slimy. Even with the few seconds I caught of him on her laptop screen, I can tell he's pretty sleazy, like one of those guys who never play by the rules, but always gets what he wants. I hate that kind of guy.

I slam the gearshift into park and stomp toward the door of In a Jam. Andie is sweeping the floor when I open the door with a huff.

"Bad day?" she asks as she leans on the broom.

"You could say that." Slumping down in a booth, I bang my head on the table. "She's. Getting. Under. My. Skin."

"Who?" Andie asks, sitting across from me, waiting as I whimper into the linoleum table.

I sit up to face her. "Jackie."

She bites her lower lip like she's trying not to smile. "She seems nice."

I lean back into the booth and growl. "Why am I torturing myself?"

"What do you mean?"

Squeezing my eyes closed, I say, "I asked her to dinner."

"Like on a date?"

When I get the nerve to open my eyes, I catch Andie doing a happy dance in her seat.

"No. Not a date. I'm going over to Silas and Marlo's tomorrow, and I figured she would like a change of scenery."

Andie sits quietly, and it drives me crazy. I tug on the neck of my T-shirt because it sure feels hot in this café. "Okay, maybe it is a date. But that is very bad."

"Why?"

"Because she has a boyfriend."

She shrugs. "Pfft. Yeah right. She seems to be an honest person, and girls like that don't flirt with guys if they have a boyfriend. Jackie has been flirting it up with you from the get-go. She seems really sweet and even interviewed me for her article. She asked a lot of questions about my grandmother and the shop and how I ended up here. She actually sounded interested."

If Andie knew Jackie's real motives, she might not think of her the same way. "It must be because I almost got her killed."

She grimaces as she wipes the table. "I heard about that. Not that I read the blog or anything. Word does travel fast in this town."

I let out a chuckle.

"I think it's more than that."

I cock my head to the side. "What do you mean?"

She takes my hands in hers and gives them a squeeze. "You've been super mopey ever since Mel left." Andie pries my fists open, and I didn't realize they were in two tightly clenched balls. "We all thought you two would get together at some point, and that might have been part of the problem. Your friends kept pushing you two together, and it just wasn't meant to be. It took her leaving the country for it to sink in to you and all of us. Maybe Jackie stirs something in you as a reminder that you're not dead. You're a good guy, Mitch. You're kind and handsome and so smart."

"Thanks for not saying 'stud.' It makes me so uncomfortable when people say that." I do a whole-body shiver.

She slides back into the booth, releasing my hands. "I'm sure it's so hard being a total catch. Must be rough." Andie snaps her fingers under my nose, making me jump. "I think I figured it out."

"What? That maybe I should get as pudgy as Stanley to keep people from calling me that name?"

"No, please don't do that. I think I know why Jackie gets to you. She's intelligent. I've heard you say more than once you thought Mel was sexy because she was smart."

Nothing sexier than a smart woman. I have said and thought that more times than I want to admit.

Andie stands and picks up her broom again. "And you have to admit, Jackie is *very* easy on the eyes."

When I avoid eye contact with her, Andie giggles. "So you *have* noticed."

"Yeah, she's..."

She points the broom at me. "Mel is practically my family now, but she was too busy trying to prove something to everyone." Andie pokes me with the end of the broom. "You have to move on. Jackie isn't Mel, and that's a good thing."

"I don't know if I'm ready, even if she is single."

"If she had a boyfriend, she would not have accepted your 'nondate' invitation."

She has a point.

"You'll never know unless you try. Have some fun, Mitch. And if fun turns into something more, Atlanta isn't *that* far away."

I hold my hands out to stop her matchmaking. "Back it up a bit, Andie. I'm just helping her with her story."

Liar.

Andie places the broom in the closet. "Denial." She waves me off. "That doesn't mean you can't have fun. Life is short. Plus, the Jackson sisters need some more material for their blog."

And with that, I'm heading upstairs. "Thanks, Andie. And for the record, I'm glad you moved here."

Her face beams with joy, like she's remembering her first days in this town. "It was the best decision I ever made."

She changed Gunnar's life. When I didn't think he would ever recover from the hell his ex-fiancée put him through and how far down the rabbit hole he fell, Andie rode into town and took his breath away and stole his heart.

"Night, Mitch."

As I settle in for the night, I check my phone for messages. I chuckle under my breath when I see Jackie left me a message. I was wondering when she would discover I entered my number into her phone while I was taking a picture of Stanley. By the timestamp, the message was sent right after I left her room.

Jackie: *You should be a detective. Very slick adding your number in my phone without me knowing.*

Me: *One of my many talents.*

Jackie: *Brett is a coworker. Nothing more.*

Jackie: *He's like a bratty brother to me.*

Jackie: *I've never even swapped spit with him.*

That one makes me chuckle, and I'm relieved. She doesn't have to explain anything to me. He might be just a colleague, or he might be more—it's none of my business. But for some reason, her need to clarify things confuses me more.

My thumbs hover over the keyboard as I search for the appropriate response. I decide to keep it light.

Me: *Good, because my image of you would be sorely tainted if THAT is the type of guy you are attracted to.*

Immediately, she replies with an eye-roll emoji.

Jackie: *That is not even close to what I consider sexy.*

I can't let that go. Me: *Do tell, ma'am.*

Jackie: *A man in a uniform. A man who can handle a crisis. A man with an easy smile. Oh, and bonus points for if he knows how to bait a hook. Do you know anyone like that?*

My cheeks hurt from grinning so much.

Me: *If I find someone that meets your description, I will send him your way.*

Jackie: *Ha. You do that. So, Smithville Stud...*

I laugh out loud at her words. She already knows how to get to me.

Jackie: *What is your type?*

While I mull over her words, I think back to my conversation with Andie. Looks aside, I do love a woman with a brain.

Before I can talk myself out of it, I reply: *Nothing sexier than a smart woman.*

The silence is deafening. Maybe I scared her off. In fact, that might be a good thing. But damn, that brain of hers, plus her looks and her curvy body—it's almost too much to handle. If I could just convince her to keep the hospital open, even when she leaves Smithville, there will be no hard feelings. That's going to be a tall order.

Right when I think the conversation is over, she sends me another text.

Jackie: *I have waited my entire life to hear those words from a man. And for them to come from you... sigh. Signed, Elmer.*

I'm so doomed.

CHAPTER NINETEEN

Jackie

When I'm barely out of the shower, someone knocks on my door. My heart does a thumpity thump in my chest because it's probably Mitch on the other side. I'm so glad Brett didn't mess up my plans. I'm at day five in Smithville, and it's already feeling way too much like home.

"Coming," I say, tugging on my jeans. Mitch said it was super casual, and he better not be pranking me. If I show up to a cotillion in denim, he will live to regret it.

Swinging open my door, I lose my breath. I've seen Mitch in his uniform and Mitch in cargo shorts, but there's something to be said about a man who can fill out a nice pair of jeans riding low on his hips. They are just the right combination of baggy and fitting. His baseball-style T-shirt stretches with every move he makes, and I'm beginning to think he wears that baseball cap everywhere, maybe even to sleep.

I don't need to think about Mitch and sleeping right now, but when he flashes me that crooked smile, I melt. "Hey there." His Southern twang washes over me, and I go weak in the knees. *Talk about swoon.*

"Hey." I could kick myself for sounding so breathless.

"I hope you don't mind, but Marlo needs us to pick up some items for dinner. She didn't get a chance to go, with the new baby and all."

"No problem at all. Do you want to take my car?"

He belts out a laugh. "I couldn't get one leg in that thing."

"It gets great gas mileage."

"So, I hear. Did you clear this little outing with your... coworker?"

I snatch his baseball cap off his head. "Let's get something straight. Brett is an old family friend and a coworker. Nothing more. I promise."

He stares down at his feet. "So it's safe to assume the sock puppets weren't for him?"

I spit out a laugh. "Not at all. Brett loves to get under my skin."

He chuckles and yanks his cap out of my hand. "I know someone else like that."

I feign ignorance. "Who? Me?" I bat my eyes for extra emphasis.

"Yep. And feisty too. However, that doesn't begin to describe you." Mitch opens the passenger door for me. "Irascible or cantankerous is more like it."

My jaw drops as I pop him in the stomach. "Watch it, Mr. Sorrow. Aren't you supposed to be impressing me?"

I wink, and his grin grows huge. "Not sure what it would take to impress you."

As I settle into the passenger seat, I say, "I'm not sure either, but a homecooked meal is a good place to start."

He puts the truck into drive. "Duly noted."

We drive down Main Street, passing the Piggly Wiggly. I point out the window. "Does Marlo not like that grocery store?"

He grins as he looks over at me. "Sure, the Pig is fine for normal stuff, but for the good stuff and for bulk items, she shops at Costco."

"Oh, impressive. I didn't know Smithville had something like that."

"We don't. It's in Albany."

"But that's..."

"Yep. An hour's drive. Forty-five if you know the back roads."

While I stare out the passenger window at the passing landscape, I ponder over what it must be like to not be able to just zip over to the nearest Trader Joe's or Whole Foods. "Do you have to do this often?"

"Most of the time, the boys just want chicken nuggets or mac and cheese, so she stocks up on that when she does a run once a month. But when I suggested we might have a guest tonight, she got all discombobulated." In a girly voice, he adds, "I'm not gonna have a guest come to my house and eat like she's at the Hamburger Hut."

"She didn't have to go out of her way. I'm sure she has her hands full as it is. I would be happy with a burger."

"Cooking makes her happy, and I was hoping you weren't one of those slick city girls that eat only organic, gluten-free, sugar-free, taste-free food."

When I cringe, he laughs. "Okay, when you put it that way, it sounds ridiculous. In fact, truth be told, I have stopped by In a Jam the last few mornings for breakfast. Mrs. Cavanaugh makes the best biscuits and jam I have ever eaten."

He snaps his head around to stare at me. "What time?"

"After you have already left for work, apparently. Mrs. Cavanaugh makes it a point to let me know you're not around."

Mitch stares out the windshield and chews on his lip. "You must think it's lame I live there."

"On the contrary. It's seriously cool, if you ask me. I'd kill to have an apartment like that in Atlanta."

"It's pretty sweet and so much quieter than living with my—" He stops his sentence, and a red flush creeps up his neck.

"It's no shame to live with family. I would if my parents would let me."

"Why won't they let you?"

I let out a groaning breath and reply, "Because I'm expected to live the part of a successful attorney. Can't be living in my parents' basement like some video game guy who can't find a job."

Mitch snorts. "Well, I never could afford video games growing up, so my reason for living with my brother was a bit more... out of necessity. Let's just say I didn't grow up anywhere near Druid Hills."

"Or as you called it, Snooty Hills."

The corner of his mouth twitches as he turns onto a highway. "Truth hurts."

I smack him on the shoulder, and he feigns pain. "What was that for?"

"I am not a snob. Trust me, I work and live around plenty of them, so I know one when I see one. In fact..."

When my sentence trails off, he glances over to me. "Go on."

"Nothing." He doesn't need to know how shallow most of my colleagues are. I love the work, but the people are very corporate *all* the time.

We ride in silence for a long time until, out of the blue, I say, "Can I ask you a question? You can say it's none of my business if you don't feel like answering."

"That sounds dangerous, but go on."

This may be the last topic he wants to talk about, especially with me, but it's been buzzing around in my brain ever since I rode with him in the ambulance. I blow out a breath. "Who is Mel? I heard Stanley say something about her, and before that, Jolene mentioned it when I was in the ER. You kind of shut her down."

The death grip he has on the steering wheel makes me think I struck a nerve. "Just somebody that used to live here."

"Everyone seems to know her. And Stanley asked for her at the hospital, so I'm guessing she was or is pretty special."

"She *is* Gunnar's cousin, and she *was* one of the ER docs at the hospital before she... up and left."

There is so much more to that answer than he's saying, and I just have to know more. "Was she your—"

"Nope. Next topic."

"Okay, remind me again—why do we have to drive all the way out here for food?"

"It's what we have to do sometimes. Imagine what it would be like to make this trek every day for work. That's what happens when a business closes in Smithville."

His words sink deep into my heart. "So this trip has nothing to do with dinner. You could have gotten steaks from the Piggy Wiggly, but you wanted to prove a point. Am I right?"

Mitch shrugs, and his mouth spreads into a wide grin. "Marlo did want to cook something special for our guest, but I may have suggested some things I knew she'd need from Costco."

I cross my arms over my chest and huff. "You don't play fair."

He throws his head back and belts out a laugh. "This isn't a game, sweetheart. Not to me or to anyone else at the hospital. And you should thank me. Marlo wanted to make a pecan pie, but I told her you were allergic."

On instinct, I reach for my throat, remembering the constricted feeling from just a few days earlier. "Have you told anyone the real reason I'm here?"

"That's not for me to tell, but Regina is one sharp cookie. If anyone can figure it out, it will be her. They all buy that story about you being a reporter, so bear with them if they romanticize this town a bit more than it is."

Each day I spend with Mitch makes it harder to stay objective about my task. This town is charming, and the residents are incredibly welcoming and lovable, one in particular.

CHAPTER TWENTY
Mitch

I think I may have bitten off more than I can chew with Jackie. My brain screams, "Run away!" But every time I decide to despise her, she does the cutest things, like snatching my baseball cap off my head or dancing in the produce section in Costco.

She did not care who was watching when "Living on a Prayer" blasted over the store speakers. She just said, "Oh my gosh, I love this song," then danced around me and pretended to have a microphone while she belted out the chorus. I'm still grinning about how carefree she acted. When the song was over, I clapped, then she bowed. My heart betrayed me by loving the moment a bit too much.

I pull up to Silas's small brick ranch home, which has seen better days, and cut the engine of my truck. "This is home." Feeling insecure about my meager upbringing, I add a disclaimer. "I know it's nothing like what you're probably used to, but... there's a lot of memories in this ratty house, good and bad. It's where we grew up, and now Silas lives here."

She nods, taking it all in. If she notices the gutter that has come loose from the roof at the corner of the house, she doesn't mention it. Nor does she comment on the peeling paint or the graveyard of riding toys behind the carport. "Don't be ashamed. It looks homey. And bigger doesn't always mean better. You know, overcompensating, like your truck."

"Ha. You're so wrong about that, but thanks anyway."

I hand her one bag of groceries and the pack of Corona Extra while I grab the cooler of meat.

"By the way, how did you know Corona was my favorite?"

"It was either that or Blackstone's Nut Brown Ale."

She lets out a giggle. "Are you trying to get rid of me?" I wish she didn't add that cute wink to her sarcasm, because that's way too hard to resist.

"You'll know when I'm trying to get rid of you."

Jackie nudges me with her shoulder. "Oh, it's the 'it's not you, it's me' speech, or maybe the 'can't we just be friends?'"

When I don't answer, she turns on a dime, her mouth hanging open. "Oh, my word. That's what happened."

Focusing on the cooler, I reply, "Not sure what you mean."

With a stern face, Jackie looks me in the eye. "With Mel. It's her loss. Big time."

The front door flies open, and Silas greets us, interrupting our uncomfortable conversation. "Hey, brother. Thanks for getting the groceries. That helped out so much."

"Jackie, this is my older brother, Silas. He was working the day of the festival, so that's why poor Marlo was on rascal duty all by herself."

Silas holds out a hand, and Jackie shakes it. "You must be the lady Mitch almost killed. Nice to meet you, Jackie. Come in."

I slap him in the gut. "Thanks, Si. Love you too."

He motions over his shoulder. "We're all out back. Clint bought the boys a plastic horseshoe set, and they're beating the snot out of him."

"Clint is..."

"The baby brother. The baseball has-been."

"Oh yeah."

"I heard that," Clint yells, coming in from the backyard. "I can still whip your butt at T-ball."

"You want to bet on it?"

"You're on. After we eat, you're going to put your money where your mouth is, because we're going to have us a good old-fashioned whiffle ball game."

"I love whiffle ball." Jackie throws her hands in the air, making Clint cock his head to the side.

He points to Jackie. "She's on my team."

Her grin couldn't get any bigger.

I lean over and whisper in her ear, "I need to warn you—we take our sports very seriously."

I also take my family very seriously. It was a big gamble bringing her here, but she seems to fit right in.

"I need to warn *you*—I take *everything* seriously."

While we eat our steaks, Jackie sits between Carson and Caleb, letting them chatter on and on. They are enamored with this new person and are mostly behaving. They have eaten off her plate a handful of times, but she doesn't flinch. In fact, she nibbled some of their fries in return. While she's not watching, I snap a photo of the three of them with my phone. Maybe, if she's nice to me, I'll send it to her.

"Marlo, this steak is better than anything I've ever had in Atlanta."

Marlo beams from the compliment. "It's all in the spices."

"You'll have to share your secret. No nuts, I assume."

Silas belts out a laugh. "You caused quite a stir at the festival, I hear. In fact, I read on the—"

I give my brother a stern stare telling him to zip it, and thank goodness he snaps his mouth shut. Jackie glances between us, then focuses back on the twins.

With Regina on his lap, Clint says, "Did Mitch tell you that we used to be pretty darn mean to him when he was little?"

She turns to me with a grin. "No, but I'd love to hear more."

With a mouth full of steak, I shrug, trying to blow it off.

Silas chuckles. "We used to tell him that he had to eat the fortune in the fortune cookie if he wanted it to come true."

Jackie covers her mouth with her hand. "Tell me you didn't believe that."

"For five years, they had me eating paper."

After she recovers from a round of giggles, she says, "My sister had me convinced I was adopted because my mother lost my birth certificate in a move."

"Harsh."

I point to Silas. "But I got him back. He hates bugs, so I would catch crickets and worms and tack them to his door. It would freak him out every single time."

Silas does a full-body shiver, making Regina giggle so much, she almost falls off Clint's lap.

Jackie's mouth drops open, then she turns to the twins. "Can you believe your uncle would do such a thing?"

Carson turns to Caleb. "Let's go catch some crickets."

They race off, and I point to Silas. "Payback, brother."

"If I have one bug in my house..."

I laugh at him. "He also told me that coins were more valuable than dollars because bills were made of plain old paper. Our father would give me a dollar, and they would convince me I should trade it to them for a nickel."

"And you believed him?"

I throw my hands into the air. "I think I was six. What do you expect?"

Without a mother to manage the roost, the inmates were definitely running the asylum. After a sip of my beer, I peek over at Jackie, who acts like she belongs, and that makes me all twitchy. She and Marlo are chatting about something while Regina checks her phone.

Regina's eyebrows scrunch together, then she clears her throat. "Jackie, I can't remember. Who do you work for again?"

Jackie side-eyes me, and I can see the nervousness in her expression. "*The Atlanta Post*," she answers, but at the same time, I say, "*Atlanta Journal*."

Jackie stares at me as she adds, "It's the *Post*, silly."

"I heard you wrote for *Country Magazine*," Marlo says, as she picks up Chloe from her Pack-n-Play.

Regina nods and stares at me. "Oh. That makes sense, I guess. Just curious."

She's not curious. Regina is honing in on something, and the last thing I need is for her to blow things for the hospital.

Clapping my hands together with more enthusiasm than is necessary, I ask, "Who's up for a game of whiffle ball?"

Carson and Caleb come running like a herd of buffalo and raise their hands. "Me."

Jackie mimics them by raising her hand. "Me too!"

"Let's go."

As everyone rises and starts to pick teams, Regina holds back and mumbles next to me, "What's up, Mitch?"

"Later. Just play along, okay?"

Regina stares at me for the longest time then gives her head a slight shake. "Be careful."

"What does that mean?"

With a whisper, she stares at Jackie while she speaks to me. "I'm not sure what's up with her, but I know you. You can't lie to get out of a parking ticket."

"I don't have to when my best friend is a cop."

"Ha-ha." She walks away and rushes up to Clint. He wraps his arm around her waist and pulls her in for a hug. Showing his feelings has always come easy to him, but it's never come naturally to me. I have more compassion for strangers than the average Joe, but emotions like love, adoration, and true happiness are foreign to me. I blame my parents for not caring more. If not for Silas, Clint and I would have been sent off to live with foster parents, and that would have devastated us all.

Jackie puts two fingers in her mouth and lets out a whistle, knocking me out of my fog. "You coming?"

I jog toward her. "Did I tell you the rules?"

She plants her hands on her hips and huffs. "I know how to play whiffle ball."

"Well, the Sorrow rule is there are no rules." I lower my voice and add, "You have been warned."

Jackie snatches my baseball cap off my head and places it on hers with a cheesy grin. "Rules are for sissies. Let's do this."

CHAPTER TWENTY-ONE

Jackie

While little Chloe rests on the sidelines in her swing and cheers us along with her baby babbles, we play a game of four-on-four whiffle ball. Silas and Mitch, along with Regina and Carson, play against Clint, Caleb, Marlo, and me. One amendment to the no-rules rule is that Clint has to play with his right arm tied to his side. Otherwise, it would be an unfair advantage. Even though he can throw better with his left than the rest of us can with our good arms, it's better than getting creamed by the ball or having him hit the whiffle ball into the neighbor's trees. I'm glad he's on my team—that's for sure.

I can't remember the last time I laughed so much that I almost peed my pants. Mitch's family tosses me into the fray like I've always been part of their crew, and while I wait for my turn to bat, I become a little misty-eyed when I get a glimpse of what an easy-going home life looks like. The way Marlo and I giggle, it's like we've known each other for years. I hope Marlo isn't too disappointed when I leave in a few days. I hope *I'm* not too disappointed either.

With Caleb on first base due to Silas's fake bobble, I point the bat at Mitch and say, "This is coming your way, Stud."

His jaw drops, and before he can recover, I whack the ball. It slides through the grass right between his legs.

Marlo yells, "Run, Caleb, run," sounding like Jenny from *Forrest Gump*. His little legs have him churning around second base as fast as he can go, but I'm right behind him. I pick him up by his armpits, his legs still spinning as he air-runs with me.

Mitch tosses the ball to Regina, who bobbles it before she recovers. She races after us, but backs off to let Caleb stomp on the cardboard box we're using as home plate. When I touch home plate, I scoop Caleb up and smother him with kisses as he lets out another round of giggles.

"Aunt Jackie, will you come back tomorrow and play?"

Like a punch to the gut, I watch his family freeze as we try to process his words and what they mean. I feel the pressure of all of their stares on me as I wait to see how Mitch reacts.

I give Caleb an Eskimo kiss and say, "Regina is your aunt, but if I can, I'll come by tomorrow to play some more."

Caleb pouts and crosses his arms. "Celeste has three aunts. How come I can only have one?"

My heart thumps against my ribcage as I sputter on my words. "I don't know the rules."

Regina takes him from me and covers his face with kisses. "It's because I used up all the awesomeness available for one family."

"Ahh." Caleb seems satisfied as he wiggles out of her grip to run off in search of his brother. I guess the game's over, especially since all the adults appear worn out and could use a hefty dose of alcohol, especially after *that* comment.

I keep my head down as I help to pick up the bats and balls, but when I hear Chloe's sweet gurgling noises, I'm drawn to her like a magnet. After unstrapping her from her swing, I pick her up and rest her sweet head on my shoulder. Her head bobbles twice before she plops it back down against my neck. Her soft skin and baby-fresh scent are sending my hormones into overdrive, and I don't mind it in the least. I can't remember feeling like this when my niece was born, but I was so busy climbing the corporate ladder, I missed most of the newborn days.

"Isn't she the cutest?" Regina asks, coming up to stand beside me.

"So cute." I plant a gentle kiss on top of Chloe's head. Her fine hair is so fine, I see her little soft spot pulsating right in my face.

Regina draws her hand down Chloe's back, and with a tender smile, she sighs. "I want one so bad, I can hardly stand it."

"Oh. You can't have any?"

She laughs. "Nothing like that. We have to get married first... again. That's the least I can do for my preacher daddy this time around."

I cock my head to the side. "Not what I was expecting, but okay."

"It's a long story, one I'm sure is way more boring than you're used to hearing. I bet as a *journalist*, you hear all sorts of crazy stories."

"Are you hogging my niece?" Mitch's voice comes from behind me, and I feel it down to my toes. He reaches out to scoop Chloe from my arms and brushes my chest in the process, sending a warm sensation through my body. He kisses Chloe where I just kissed her, and now I can't stop staring at his perfect lips. "Chloe, sweetie, we had a deal. It's you and me against the world."

Regina laughs as she walks away. When she reaches Clint, he leans down to give her a piggyback ride, and a twinge of sadness rushes through me. I want what she has. Not the guy, but what she has with the right guy.

"Are you okay?"

Shaking my head, I swallow hard, then I nod. "I'm just tired."

"We can leave. I have to work early tomorrow anyway." He returns Chloe to her mother and takes my hand. "Jackie and I are going to head out. Thanks for everything."

Marlo kisses his cheek then turns to me. She grabs me into a side hug and whispers, "Mitch needs someone like you in his life. Please don't break his heart."

Mitch scrunches his eyebrows together as if he's trying to figure out what Marlo said to me, but I plaster on my lawyer face I've perfected over the years, even though I'm a mess inside.

"Thank you for inviting me and for sharing your..." I stare around at the craziness happening all over the backyard, doing my dead-level best not to ugly cry. Silas and Clint wrestle with the boys while Regina acts as the referee, favoring the little ones. As Chloe nestles safely in her mother's arms, I say, "Thanks for inviting me."

Mitch squeezes my hand as he leads me back to his truck. He drops my hand to open the door, and I already miss his warm, rough skin.

"By the way, you're not getting your cap back. You do know that, right?"

He grins as he fakes an attempt to snatch it off my head. "I kind of figured that."

Riding in silence, I relive the evening, and the tears start to pool in my eyes. To keep Mitch from seeing the tears I'm no longer able to hold back, I pretend to focus on all the photos I've taken over the last few days, but my eyes are so blurry, I can't see anything on the screen.

He rests a hand on my knee. "Are you okay?" His voice is soft and filled with concern.

Swiping away a stray tear, I nod. "Peachy."

He chuckles. "For an attorney, you're a terrible liar."

"I'm usually good at having a poker face, but this is different." I suck in my breath, hoping I can get my emotions in check.

"I'm sorry if my family upset you or if the lying is getting to you—"

"It's not that."

Mitch puts his truck in park in front of the inn and turns to look at me, concern etched across his face. "Go on."

And like a geyser erupting, tears pour from my eyes. I cover my face with my hands and say through my crying jag, "I loved every minute of it."

"You got a funny way of showing it."

I snort out a laugh as I open the door to his truck. He follows me to the front door of the inn. I stare at the ground, hoping to gain control of my emotions, and whisper, "Thank you for today."

"You're welcome. I, uh, took some pictures of you." He scratches the back of his neck.

"I noticed."

"You know... for your article."

I stare off in the distance. "I never had anything like that growing up."

"I'm not following you."

"Don't get me wrong. My parents love me, and I enjoy spending time with them, but I never had *that*. The laughing, razzing each other, playing games, feeling completely consumed by love..."

I stare up at him, and without putting much thought into it, I stand on my tiptoes, place my hands on his forearms for support, and plant a quick kiss on his lips. They are even softer than I imagined.

I should *not* have done that.

Mitch's eyes grow big, and I back away.

"I'm so sorry. That was inappropriate." I turn on a dime and fidget with my lock.

He lets out a sexy growl. "Aw, what the hell."

Turning me around, he pulls me close. One arm slips around my waist while the other hand cradles my head. I let out a gasp as our bodies press together. He slams his lips to mine, and this time, it's not a quick peck. It's passionate and sensual, and he knows what he's doing. My knees go weak, and he tightens his grip around my waist while continuing with this massive make-out session. I wrap my arms around his neck, not wanting it to end. When his kisses trail down my neck, then back to my mouth, I no longer have two working brain cells left.

When we come up for air, I feel like I could fly. I adjust the baseball cap on my head and whisper, "I should go. Thanks for the kiss. I mean for the..." I point to the front door as I back toward it. "I better let you go before I..." *Gah!* "Goodbye, Mitch."

He laughs as he walks backward. *You are such a dork. You* thanked *him for the kiss?*

He wipes a hand over his mouth.

"Are you wiping that kiss away?"

"Nope. Rubbing it in. See you later, Myers."

I rush to him and take his face in my hands to plant one last hard kiss on his lips. "Good night."

With a wink and a nod, he saunters away, and I'm left wondering how I got into this situation. I'm supposed to figure out a way to shut down the hospital and send Mitch and the rest of the staff to the unemployment line, not fall for him.

The best I can do now is to discover specific examples in the data to justify keeping the hospital open while I try to refrain from getting too attached to the Smithville Stud. I don't think either is going to happen, because I have thoroughly and completely fallen head over heels with him. And by the way he kissed me back, he feels the same.

Now what?

CHAPTER TWENTY-TWO
Mitch

At a snail's pace, I slog into In a Jam, eyes trained on the floor. Andie counts money at the cash register, and I feel her gaze on me as I climb the stairs to my apartment. I flop down on the couch and stare at the ceiling, thinking about Jackie's lips on mine and our bodies pressed together, fitting like a glove. One more second, and my restraint would have been out the window. I'm a fool for getting so close to her when I clearly know her intentions. It's one thing to show her around the town, and it's even fine for her to hang with my family, but tongue wrestling with her is a whole different level.

I don't know what I've gotten myself into.

A quiet knock comes to my door. "Mitch, it's me, Andie. Can I come in?"

With a whimper, I sit up. "Door's unlocked."

She gingerly enters the room and sits next to me on the couch. "What's going on?"

I finally glance her way and lie through my teeth. "Nothing. Just tired."

Andie waggles a finger in front of my face. "Your eyes look stormy today."

"Huh?"

"Normally, your eyes are very bright. But today, you look..." She shrugs. "I don't know, maybe weary. Do you feel like talking to someone who hasn't known you your entire life?"

Squeezing the heels of my hands into my eye sockets, I let out a groan. "Why am I only attracted to unobtainable women?"

128

"Is this about Mel?"

I shake my head. "That ship has sailed, and I'm finally okay with it, but you would think I could learn."

"Jackie?"

"Yep. She kissed me, and I could have let it go, but then... I kissed her back."

I'm so glad she's not laughing at me, because I don't think I could take it.

"What makes you think she's not obtainable? Is she married?"

I let out a laugh. "No, at least I don't think so. And to be completely honest, it wasn't just a little peck on the cheek. I kissed her like my life depended on it."

"Maybe it does."

Does it? Covering my face with my hands, I sit in silence for a moment. Andie doesn't say anything. The only sound I hear is my heart beating.

Andie clears her throat to get my attention. "Do you think she's out of your league?"

"Possibly. But there's more. Can you keep a secret? I have to talk to someone about this."

Andie runs her thumb and finger over her mouth as if to zip it shut, making me grin. I'm so glad she came into Gunnar's life—and all of our lives, for that matter.

After a large swallow, I say, "Jackie is not a journalist."

"I figured as much. What is she doing here, and why all the secrecy?"

I slump back into the couch and stare at the ceiling. "She's an attorney for the hospital organization Smithville Regional is part of. She's here to see if it needs to be shut down."

Her mouth forms an O as she ponders my words. "Are you sure? How did you find that out?"

"She let it slip when I took her to the ER after her allergic reaction to my pie, which, by the way, doesn't help matters."

Andie stands and paces the living room, then she picks up a picture of her grandmother, the original owner of the building. Andie kept the place decorated with her grandmother's pictures, and I'm guessing it's to remind her of the tie she has to the community. She shoves the picture in my face. "The corporation can't close the hospital. Without the caring staff, my grandmother would have died a long time ago. People like you took care of her when I didn't even know she was still alive. Jackie can't let this happen. She just can't."

"I know. During the day, she reviews the data about the hospital, complaints, and stuff like that. But we made a deal. She has given me a week to convince her it needs to stay open. So far, all I've been able to do is show her around town and get way too close to her. Actually, I think I've made things worse."

Andie sits next to me and clasps my hands in hers. "Don't you understand? That's exactly what she needs to see. Data only shows the superficial facts. It's the people and their connections to the hospital that you're showing her."

"I still shouldn't have kissed her."

She waves off my comment. "That's a totally different issue. Tell me something. What about her is so alluring, other than the sexy-brain thing?"

Chuckling, I think back over the last few days. So much about Jackie draws me to her like a bee to nectar. "It's hard to pinpoint one thing, but she's feisty. I do like that."

Andie grins and waggles her eyebrows. "I've noticed."

"I guess if I had to find one thing about her that stands out, it's that she accepts my family just as they are. It's almost like she's always been around them. She doesn't look down on us because we're less educated or have smaller bank accounts. Although, Clint's net worth is a definite outlier in our little group. But the kicker is the way she interacts with my niece... She glows when she holds Chloe."

"Like you do."

I dip my head in bashful agreement.

Andie glances around the apartment then cocks her head to the side. "Where's your baseball cap? The one Clint gave you."

The corner of my mouth twitches, and Andie adds, "Oh my gosh. I hate to tell you this, but you're a goner. Nothing says love like a country boy giving his baseball cap to a girl."

I scrub my face with my hands. "You make it sound like I presented it to her like my class ring or something. And, I didn't *give* it to her. She snatched it off my head and took possession of it."

Andie pats the top of my head like I'm a little puppy. "But did you ask for it back?"

"Not necessarily."

"Ha! Told ya."

"Andie, it doesn't matter. The kiss was a fluke."

"Kisses. Plural."

"Okay, kisses. I really think she was consumed with baby hormones when she kissed me."

"Then I'm glad it stopped at a few kisses. It did stop there, right?"

Thinking about how I wish the answer was different, I feel my ears burn. "Yes. Nothing else happened."

I head into the kitchenette in search of a snack. Flinging open the refrigerator, I welcome the cool air. Maybe that will chill my hormones. "I'm sure she's already regretting it. I mean, what would I have to offer her except a fling, and I don't do flings."

She slides past me and makes herself at home by grabbing a Diet Coke out of the refrigerator. "Mitch, you are jumping off the dock. Back up. Enjoy life. And stop thinking for someone else. That will get you in a world of hurt faster than the Jackson sisters can blog."

I smack my hand with my other fist. "Shit. The blog. God, I hope they don't get wind of the kiss. That's all I need. We can kiss the hospital goodbye. Pun intended."

Andie grimaces. "Their eyes are everywhere, so be prepared."

"And if Jackie thinks we're all a bunch of gossips, it will be just as bad."

"Life in a small town was hard to get used to at first, but eventually, I made peace with the gossipy part of it. It's a small price to pay for a real family."

My phone chirps, and I pull it out from my pocket. My heartbeat picks up the pace when I see who's messaging me. "It's from Jackie." I grin when I read her text.

"What does it say? I'm as nosy as the next person."

"She says, 'About that kiss. Sorry not sorry.'"

Andie hip bumps me. "Told ya. I'm out of here. Just have fun, Mitch. You deserve to have some fun. You've spent your entire life running from your parents' reputation. You're not them. Enjoy life. Okay?"

God love her, she's a breath of fresh air in this town. "Yes, ma'am."

"I'm leaving, and I promise I won't tell a soul, not even Gunnar."

"Thank you."

When she closes the door, I slump back down on the couch and text Jackie back.

Me: *I'm not sorry either.*

Jackie: *I still have to remain objective in my job.*

A little deflated, I text back: *Of course.*

After a moment of silence, another message comes in, and it makes me beam with happiness.

Jackie: *I like you Mitch. A lot. Thank you for today. And. Gah. I have never felt this way about anyone. Ever!*

When I think my grin can't get any bigger, it does.

Me: *I like you too. And ditto on the feelings.*

She sends me a smiley face emoji with heart eyes and another one wearing a baseball cap. *I also like my cap. Don't you think I look 'fetch'?*

She's so adorable.

Me: *Very much so.*

Jackie: *Goodnight, Sorrow.*

Me: *Sweet dreams, Myers.*

As I settle in for the night, I relive our kisses. I've kissed lots of girls, and this is by far the most passionate kiss I have ever had. It was like she was drowning, and I was saving her. Or maybe it was the other way around. I might be the one who needs saving. If so, I'm not sure why the person with the life preserver has to be the one who's trying to kill my job and change this town forever. It's the most complicated feeling I've ever had.

CHAPTER TWENTY-THREE
Jackie

Descending the stairs of the inn, I let out another huge yawn. Bobby James sits behind the front desk, reading. When he sees me, he slides the book toward me. "I took your advice and got the latest Sarah Slade novel." He fans himself. "That woman can make a sailor blush."

Grinning, I fix myself a cup of coffee. "I thought you would like that one."

"Would you like to read it after me?"

My coffee slides down my throat, giving me a welcome jolt of energy that I'll definitely need for today since I got little-to-no sleep last night while reliving Mitch's lips on mine and his strong arms holding my body. He's delicious, and I wouldn't mind more from where that came from. "Thanks, but I already read it. Do you want to know if Tessa—"

He slams his hands over his ears and yells, "La, la, la, la, la. Don't spoil it for me."

"Okay, okay. But it's a shocker. We'll talk about it when you're done."

"You got it. Oh, and, Miss Jackie, I might want to just warn you that the motion sensor on the inn might have picked up on a certain encounter last night."

I gasp. "I can explain."

He shakes his head. "No need to explain. It's none of my business. Just be more hugger mugger next time. There are no secrets in this town."

Hugger mugger? Next time? I doubt there will be a next time. There definitely doesn't need to be a second encounter, not that I would turn it away if the chance came my way.

"Thanks for the warning." I take another sip of coffee. "Have a nice day, and let me how far you get in Tessa's adventure."

With a wave, I'm out the door. Even though I could walk, I drive my Mini Cooper the two blocks to In a Jam so I don't have to walk back to the inn before going to the hospital. I would also risk running into Mitch, and I don't think I'm ready to talk to him in person after our lip-lock and fun text messages. It was all so out of character for me, and I'm a bit embarrassed about how bold I've been. Although I don't regret any of it, I at least need my breakfast first. I hide in my car until Mitch, dressed in this EMT uniform, rushes out the door on the way to his work, which is where I should be.

I know I'm a chicken for waiting for him to leave, but I don't trust myself around him. My lips would want to be attached to his as soon as I was within five feet of him.

Once Mitch's truck turns the corner, I let out a sigh of relief and enter the building.

"Morning, Miss Jackie. I have your breakfast all ready." Mrs. Cavanaugh slides me a plate full of the most delectable biscuits and gravy I have ever laid eyes on.

"Thank you, Mrs. Cavanaugh. I'm going to gain ten pounds this week from all your good cooking, but it will be worth every ounce."

Andie walks in the door, tugs an apron off a hook, and rushes to the coffee pot to pour her a cup. "Sorry I'm late. I didn't get much sleep last night. My mind just wouldn't shut off."

"Same," I say.

Andie smiles as she pours me a cup of coffee and slides the bowl of creamers toward me. Just a few days ago, I would have wrinkled up my brow at the store-bought creamers, but it's already grown on me.

"Maybe we were thinkin' about the same thing." She takes a sip of her coffee.

"I doubt it. Mine is..."

"A man." Mrs. Cavanaugh doesn't miss a beat with the batter she's beating.

Andie cocks one eyebrow. "Now, now, Mrs. Cavanaugh. We don't gossip in here." Her eyes dart toward two elderly ladies wearing the most hideous hats I've ever seen. One hat looks like something Mary Poppins would wear and the other one is so big she could use it as an umbrella.

Mrs. Cavanaugh harrumphs.

We remain quiet, and eventually, the two old ladies stand to leave.

"Good day, Ms. Jackson, other Ms. Jackson," Andie says.

One of the old ladies does her best to be casual, but I know I heard her cell phone click like she took a picture. Once the bell chimes over the door and the ladies leave, Andie runs around the counter to sit next to me. "Okay, the coast is clear. Spill. I know that look, even if I don't know *you* very well."

I glance from her to Mrs. Cavanaugh then ask, "Did that woman just take a picture of me?"

"Probably." Andie waves off my shock. "She may be old, but she can run circles around any teenager when it comes to modern technology. Twitter, Instagram... It wouldn't surprise me if she's on TikTok."

"Wow."

"And that blog..." Mrs. Cavanaugh mumbles.

Andie shushes Mrs. Cavanaugh. "Enough about them. Jackie, what happened?"

I lay my head on the counter and beat my fist on it. "I'm the worst person on the planet."

"You kissed Mitch, didn't you?" Mrs. Cavanaugh rolls out the dough on a floured surface.

I don't know if I should lie or tell them the truth—or which version of the truth.

Sopping up my biscuit with gravy, I say, "Maybe."

"Yes." Andie punches the air with her fist. Her mouth drops open in a silent squeal.

"I don't want to lead him on."

"Did he kiss you back?"

A flush creeps up my neck, and my ears are on fire. I couldn't deny it even if I wanted to. "Yep, most definitely, but remember, I'll be gone on Sunday."

Andie waves me off and looks at Mrs. Cavanaugh. "Do you know anyone else that had those same thoughts?"

Mrs. Cavanaugh points a spatula at me. "Child. Kiss him. Kiss his socks off. Kiss every stitch of clothing off that man."

I gulp down the last of my coffee, slide a few dollar bills across the counter, then toss a couple more in the tip jar. "And with that, I should probably go."

"Wait." Andie scribbles something down on a napkin and hands it to me. "There's a full moon tonight. It's tradition to go to the lake and moon bathe."

I stare down at the napkin where she wrote an address on it.

"That's where Gunnar and I live."

"We went fishing there the other day."

"Swimming, too, from what I hear," Mrs. Cavanaugh adds.

Andie rolls her eyes. "Anyway, you can park wherever and walk around to the back. Just follow the music and the bonfire. Any time after dark."

"Thanks," I say, my voice barely above a whisper. "That's so sweet of you."

Gathering my things, I blink back tears for the second day in a row. The people here are so nice. They hardly know me, and they're so kind at every turn. If they only knew my real motives for being here, they would ban me from ever stepping foot in this town again. And when Mitch realizes I'm doing all of this for a promotion, he may never speak to me again.

"It's fun. I remember my first moon bathing." She looks away with a far-off gaze in her eyes, like she's remembering every moment of that night. "It will change your life."

I simply nod before leaving the café, because if I try to reply, I might fall apart.

AFTER WALKING THE HALLWAYS of the hospital all day, I can't find even one item wrong. Maybe I'm not looking hard enough on purpose, but nothing seems noteworthy. Even in the cafeteria, I didn't overhear one single person say anything bad about the staff or the hospital. Unable to find anything physical to add to my report, I head back to my room and log in to the systems, but my mind keeps circling back to Mitch.

As I review the human resources reports, I run across a document from a Dr. Melanie Ballard and wonder if she's the "Doc Melly" Mitch is so opposed to talking about. I can't believe what I'm reading. Apparently, Dr. Ballard pulled Mitch out of his ambulance EMT position and into the ER for a week while they were short-staffed. She admitted to ordering him to do some procedures out of his scope of practice. She took responsibility and recommended Mitch not be reprimanded since no harm was done to the patient. That has to be the problem between the two of them and maybe why she left town. Her last day of employment was right around the same time as the document.

I sit back and squeeze my eyes shut. This is really bad. She's no longer employed at the hospital, so no action can be taken directly against her, but the fact that the hospital administrator didn't do anything about it, whether he knew about the incident in real time or not, speaks volumes about how this hospital is run. It's a good ole boy network, and as long as no one gets hurt, people look the other way.

But rules are rules, and I can't leave this out of my report. Matthew is going to flip when he hears about this. I bet even Brett doesn't have anything this damning to report about at his hospital. Sure, he probably has more hand-washing violations, but this is huge enough to get a hospital shut down, especially one that's teetering on failure anyway.

I pick up my phone, and I'm about to send a quick message to Matthew when I pause and stare at the last few messages Mitch and I sent to each other. He's the only reason I haven't fired off an email immediately.

Maybe I shouldn't be so hasty to report this. There has to be more to the story than what was in the report. I bet Mitch has a very good explanation for the incident. Surely, he wouldn't be stupid enough to do something so big just because his girlfriend asked him to.

There's only one way to find out. I shove my phone into my purse, along with the napkin Andie gave me, and head out toward the lake to do some moon bathing. Maybe I'll get to the bottom of the Mel-and-Mitch story, both professionally and personally.

CHAPTER TWENTY-FOUR
Mitch

My boom box blasts my favorite Southern rock tunes as Clint starts the bonfire by the lake. My brain wouldn't let me sleep at all, and work did nothing to keep my mind off kissing Jackie. And watching Regina and Clint being so lovey-dovey is not making the situation any better. I'm used to it with Liza Jane and Jake, because they've been married for a good while, but now that all of my friends are paired up, I'm definitely the odd man out. And since Regina and Clint have been reunited, I am the constant fifth wheel, or more like the seventh wheel in this friend group. Liza Jane puffs on a cigarette while Gunnar and Jake laugh about something I'm not in the least bit interested in.

Andie plops down beside me and stretches her legs out, drawing her bare feet through the sand. She stares into the fire. "I remember my first moon bathing."

Liza Jane laughs. "Yep. I caught you making out with Gunnar."

Her eyes grow big. "That was not what you thought it was."

"Yes, it was." Gunnar grins.

Liza nods to her husband. "You remember, don't you?"

Jake holds up his hands in defense as he looks from Gunnar to Andie. "I'm staying out of it."

Andie sits straighter and shakes her head. "What I mean is that it was the first time I felt part of the group. It really changed me."

"It was Gunnar's lips." Liza Jane's comment makes Regina giggle so much, she rolls over into the sand.

"Hey now, don't run her off." Gunnar gets up to stand behind Andie and gives her shoulders a squeeze. "I kind of like her here."

Andie grins as she stares up at her fiancé. "You better." Her smile grows even bigger when she looks off toward her house then waves. "You came."

We all turn to find Jackie walking toward us, wearing jeans rolled up to her shins, her hair down around her shoulders, and carrying her flip-flops.

Da-um. My heartbeat quickens as she and I lock eyes. *What on earth is she doing here?*

Andie rushes toward her. "Have you met everyone? This is Liza Jane and Jake. They own the hardware store down the street from In a Jam."

Liza tosses the rest of her cigarette into the fire and shakes Jackie's hand. "Howdy. Welcome to moon bathing. It will be a life-altering event."

"And, of course, you've met Clint, Regina... and Mitch. This is Gunnar." Andie slides her arm through his and rests her head on his shoulder.

Jackie scans each of my friends and smiles at this ragtag group as she gives them all a bashful wave. "Hi. Andie invited me. I hope that's okay."

Ahh, good old matchmaker Andie. I cut my eyes toward her, and she motions with her head toward Jackie. After a deep breath, I stand and walk to Jackie.

"Hey. Glad you came." I motion toward the group. "Well, this is it. We sit around the bonfire, drink, listen to music, and forget about the world for a few hours. Exciting, huh?"

"Sounds lovely." Jackie slides a wisp of hair behind her ear.

I motion to the log I was sitting on. "You can sit here. Would you like a beer?"

Jackie sits and smiles up at me. "Just water. I drove, plus I have a low tolerance for alcohol."

"Me too," Andie says, sending the entire group into a fit of laughter.

Jackie looks around, not getting the joke. I lean over and whisper, "Andie used to be a bit of a party girl when she lived in Boston."

"Ahh," she replies, like the dynamics are clicking into place in her mind.

I hand her a bottle of water and take one for myself. The last thing I need to do is to lower my inhibitions around Jackie. And I certainly don't want her to bust my chops about drinking and driving. With a cop in the group, we always tone it down or sleep it off at his house.

Sipping her water, Jackie says, "This is very nice. It reminds me of college days when I could cut loose without my parents knowing."

Regina lifts her bottle in salute. "I hear ya, sister. My father is the preacher, so I couldn't get away with *anything* in this town."

Jackie grimaces and holds up a finger. "My father's a judge so..."

"Ooh..." Jake holds his chest like he's in pain. "That had to have been tough."

She shrugs. "I learned early on to behave, at least while under his jurisdiction."

"I don't know the meaning of *behave*." At least Liza Jane is honest.

"Me either," Clint says, tossing back the last of his beer. "But those days are over."

"Finally." Regina nudges him in the side before cozying up to him.

Gunnar stands and clears his throat, and I know what's coming. "Jackie, would you like to hear about the time—"

"No," Andie and Liza Jane yell at the same time.

Jackie blinks then turns to me. "I take it this is a story that's been told a few times."

"More than we can count."

Grinning, she motions toward Gunnar. "I'd like to hear it."

Liza Jane groans while she lights up another cigarette. She blows the smoke away from our faces. "You've been warned."

Through a fit of chuckles, Jake and Gunnar collectively tell the story of when Gunnar put his thumbs in a set of Chinese handcuffs and almost lost the feeling in his hands.

Gunnar pats my back, almost knocking me over. "But good ole Mitch saved the day."

"Woo-hoo, glory hallelujah." Liza Jane raises her hands over her head in mock celebration, making Jackie laugh.

"Hey, Mitch," Andie says, "why don't you show Jackie the trail that leads around the lake?"

Regina raises an eyebrow, but the rest of the group nods in agreement.

"Why don't we let our guest decide?" If she doesn't want to spend any alone time with me, I've just given her an out.

With a bashful grin, Jackie bows her head. "I'd love to see it, but only if you want to show it to me. I don't want to disturb your plans."

Liza belts out a laugh. "Oh, honey, you're looking at it."

Clint shoos us away. "Yeah, go on."

Regina elbows him in the ribs.

"Ow."

I stand, dust the sand off my butt, and hold out a hand for Jackie to take. "We better, or we'll be harassed all night until we do."

She takes my hand and stands. "Wouldn't want that."

With her hand still in mine, we stroll closer near the shoreline, to the far side of the lake. My friends' laughter gets fainter with every step. She rotates her hand so our fingers are laced together, a small act that warms my heart in a big way.

The water quietly laps near our ankles. In silence, I focus on our feet squishing in the wet sand. Her shoulder brushes against my arm. When the bonfire is only a tiny speck on the fire side of the lake, I turn her to face me.

She stares down at her hands, which have found their way to my waist. Sliding her thumbs through my belt loops, she stares up at me and shrugs. "I haven't been able to stop thinking about our kiss."

Yes! "Me either."

"And for the last three days, I've watched you work, spent time with your family, and now I'm hanging out with your friends. Why? Was it just so I wouldn't shut down the hospital?"

"No."

Jackie snorts and tugs on my belt loops. "A man of few words." She raises her gaze until we stare into each other's eyes. Her face glows in the moonlight like she's a goddess. "Then what is it?"

When I don't answer, she continues.

"There are some things I need to ask you..." She shakes her head. "Now isn't the time. I like you, Mitch. From the moment I first laid eyes on you, I just haven't been able to get you out of my head."

I cup her face with my hands and whisper, "I feel the same way."

When my lips touch hers, a warm sensation runs through my body, like I'm alive for the very first time. She clutches my waist tighter until our bodies are smashed together. She slides her hands up my chest, making me groan, and when she wraps her arms around my neck, I hold her so tight, she might not be able to breathe.

When we come up for air, I ask, "What are we doing?"

Panting, she replies, "I don't know, and I don't care."

"Good." My lips crash back onto hers, and I'm transported to another realm.

There was a reason Mel and I never connected—because there was someone better for me out there, someone perfect for me. And now, that someone is here. I can either take a chance with Jackie or always wonder what if. I'm tired of playing it safe.

Griff runs up to me with a stick in his mouth, forcing Jackie to take a step away from me. Already missing her contact, I let out a groan, snatch the stick out of Griff's mouth, and toss it down the beach. "I love that dog, but he has terrible timing."

She chews on her lip then says barely above a whisper, "We could... go somewhere more private."

My heart pounds out of my chest, and for the first time since I moved out of my brother's house, I'm so glad to have my own place.

"Thirty minutes. Park behind In a Jam." I waggle my eyebrows as I slide a strand of hair behind her ear.

She stares off at the lake for a moment then dips her head with a bashful smile. "I'll be there."

We walk back to my friends in silence, and I have to fight the urge to pull her in for another embrace, but I behave.

"The lake is so pretty, especially on a night like tonight." She plops down at the bonfire across from me and pokes the fire with a stick. I sink down next to my boom box and pretend to listen while Liza rambles on about how Mrs. Butterfield wanted two gallons of Ice Sculpture White paint, but she gave her the swatch of Ethereal White. Every now and then, Jackie checks her watch, and I do my best not to grin.

I'm counting the minutes, too, cutie.

Jackie lets out a huge, exaggerated yawn, complete with stretching her arms over her head. "Thanks for inviting me, but I've had a long day. I think I'm going to call it a night." She waves to the group and adds, "Goodnight."

"Would you like me to walk you to your car?" *Way to be so obvious, Sorrow.*

"No thanks. I'll be fine." She waves then gives me a quick wink.

I watch every swing of her hips until her body is out of sight. Then I hear her car start up, and when the taillights fade into the darkness, I turn to my friends.

Andie is the first to break the silence. "What are you waiting for?"

I roll my eyes, pick up my boom box, and leave my friends while Gunnar lets out a wolf whistle. I love my friends and family, but sometimes, they are a bit too meddlesome.

CHAPTER TWENTY-FIVE
Jackie

Sitting in the dark alley behind In a Jam as I review my situation, I feel like a criminal. On one hand, Mitch is the sweetest, best looking man I've ever met. And to think he likes me is beyond belief. I'm able to let my hair down, figuratively and literally, when I'm around him, and I adore everything about his family. I have fallen in love with this sleepy, small town filled with genuine people, as well as the stereotypical town gossips and their silly blog.

On the other hand, I have a very successful career waiting for me in Atlanta. I'm within striking distance of the VP position, something I've wanted and deserved for years. And Smithville Regional is just another small-town hospital that doesn't have a leg to stand on. *Eye on the prize, Jackie.*

But if the hospital closes, people will have to go at least an hour away for their health issues. Some may not be able to travel; others may not be able to afford to obtain healthcare. It's quite possible my decisions could cost some people their lives. I don't know if I'm prepared to take on that kind of guilt. Maybe it was a bad idea for Matthew to send me here. It's one thing to analyze facts on paper, but it's a different, more visceral issue when facts can't be separated from the human component.

I shake the thoughts out of my head as I drum my fingers on my steering wheel. I'm a grown woman, and I want this with Mitch, so somehow, I'll figure out a way to have both the promotion and the man.

My phone rings, scaring the crap out of me. Assuming it's Mitch, I answer, "Hey, I'm waiting for you. Where are you?"

"Uh... didn't you read the texts I sent you?" Brett's question turns the contents of my stomach to hot coals.

"What do you want?"

"I'm at your B&B waiting for you. We have to talk. Now."

"You can't be there. Leave. Immediately."

"Jacqueline, this is serious."

"I'm busy."

"Busy talking to the hospital administrator about that little issue with a certain EMT working outside his scope of practice?"

I suck in a huge breath then ask, "How do you know about that?"

He sighs. "I have access to the same information as you. Has the fresh air down there made your brain cells shrink?"

My pulse races as I do my best to calculate my options in the matter of two seconds. "I'm trying to get to the bottom of it. There is always more than one side to the story. Didn't you learn that in law school?" I suddenly realize that I never asked Mitch to explain what happened that week in the emergency room. We kind of got sidetracked with more interesting issues.

"I'm sending you Dr. Melanie Ballard's contact info. She's out of the country, but her HR records say she will have periodic cell service if anyone has an issue with a patient she treated. If you really want to be objective, give her a call."

"I don't need to bother her."

"Why? Because you're banging the EMT?"

Oh, no he didn't.

"How dare you accuse me of that? I'll be there in five minutes. Don't leave. I want to bitch you out in person. And how did you know where I was staying?" Penny would never disclose that kind of information.

Brett chuckles. "There weren't too many choices to begin with, but the big peach gave it away."

The phone is muffled, and I hear a scuffle. "Ow. Go away."

"What's going on?"

"I just got attacked by a chicken."

Wild chickens to the rescue! "Serves you right. I'll be there shortly."

Before I disconnect the call, I hear him yell, "Not the car!"

I hope there's a big pile of chicken poop, and it wouldn't hurt me any if there are scratches all over his prized possession.

I crank my car and spin out of the alley toward the Peach Fuzz Inn, ready to put Brett in his place. He doesn't get to come here unannounced and interfere in my investigation even though the facts are clear as mud.

LEANING UP AGAINST his Mercedes AMC GT, which Brett refers to as his "chick magnet," he scrolls through messages on his phone. I screech my Mini Cooper to a halt only inches from his back bumper and slam my door behind me.

"Jesus, you cannot afford to pay for a scratch on my ride. I've already had to fight off an angry hen who decided it was her new nest."

"Oh, boo-hoo. What do you want?"

He backs away from me. "When you wouldn't answer my texts, I thought I would talk to you in person. It can't wait."

As I tick off items on my hand, I reply, "What are you doing here? Why are you spying on me? And why on earth are you spending so much time reviewing *my* hospital's stats?"

"Wow, slow down and breathe before you pass out." He puts a hand on each of my shoulders.

I shrug him off like he has the plague. "Answer my questions."

Brett glances around and says in a hushed tone, "Can we take it inside? I don't want to disturb the people who have probably been asleep since eight o'clock."

Weighing my options, I grab his arm and drag him inside before anyone sees us. I plop him down in the common living area and poke a finger in his face. "Don't mess with me. What are you up to?"

He swats my finger away and huffs. "Fine, my hospital is so boringly in order, I wanted to see what my competition was up to, and you, my dear, have a doozie. I wish I was assigned here."

I cross my arms. "I've found most things are in order. There's one tiny mishap that will be addressed tomorrow."

"Tiny mishap? That could get even a huge hospital shut down. What are you waiting for? You don't have to look any deeper. Call her if you need to. Write your report, get back to Atlanta and—"

"Why do you care so much? That it would prove I would make the perfect candidate for the VP position?"

He rolls his eyes. "Oh, please. Everyone knows you're more qualified than me, including *moi*. The promotion is yours for the taking. Just seal the deal. You had to have stumbled upon that information days ago. Matthew needs to know. Immediately."

I stumble backward in disbelief. "Did you tell him already?"

"No, I didn't, only because we're friends. But if you don't, I will." He walks closer to me, making me take a step backward. "You're already falling under the small-town spell. Your judgment is completely clouded."

I swallow hard. "That's not true. I'm just as objective as I've ever been."

Brett cocks an eyebrow. "Okay, then where were you tonight when you should have been preparing the most important report of your career?"

"None of your business, and you're just envious of me because I'm more efficient than you. It always takes you three times longer to do your reports than me, especially when Penny isn't doing them for you or if I don't proof your work."

His jaws clench, and I know I've hit a nerve. But like the Brett I've had to work with for the past few years, he's quick on his feet. "Who are you sleeping with?"

Before I realize what I'm doing, I slap his face so hard, his cell phone tumbles to the ground. "Get out of here."

"Sure." He rubs his jaw while he picks up his cell phone. As he walks toward the front door, he stops and chuckles. "I think I have my answer. Be careful, Jack."

I snap my head around to find Mitch standing there as stiff as a stone.

Brett walks past him, bumping his shoulder into Mitch's along the way. "Bye, honey."

I'm going to rip his head off the next time I see him.

My lip trembles because this scene looks so bad, and I don't even know how to explain it to Mitch. Before I can say anything, Mitch breaks the silence. "When you didn't show up, I thought maybe we had our wires crossed. I guess I misunderstood. Big time."

Right when he touches the doorknob, I reach out to him. "Mitch, let me explain. This is not what it looks like."

Mitch's face looks so sad and disappointed. "I blew off the online chat you were having with him, but I'm beginning to think there's more to this than you're letting on. He came all the way here to see you at night, and I'm supposed to think it's nothing? Don't piss on my boots and tell me it's raining. I'm not as stupid as you think I am."

"You're not stupid at all. I'm sorry. I know it looks bad, but..." I force him to sit in a chair in the lobby, and I stand in front of him, nibbling on a fingernail. "There is nothing going on with Brett. He's a dingleberry, at best."

Mitch gets a chuckle out of that term.

"I hate working with him, and he torments me all the time." Now is as good a time as ever to tell him about the incident I found and about the promotion. It will kill my chances with him, but it's the right thing to do.

Mitch nods as he stares straight ahead as if he's mulling something over in his head. "I shouldn't, but I believe you."

I let out a sigh of relief and motion toward the steps that lead to my room. "Great, because if you want to..."

He grins, but it doesn't reach his eyes. "As much fun as I know that would be, I'm not really in the mood anymore." He stands, gives me a kiss on the cheek, and leaves.

I cannot believe this blew up in my face. I pull out my phone to send Mitch a message, then I see Brett's with Dr. Ballard's number.

Blowing out a breath, I type out a message to her: *I am Jackie Dalton from the Southeastern Hospital Association. I need to speak to you about an incident that happened at Smithville Regional. Please contact me at your earliest convenience, any time.*

So, in good conscience, I've tried to reach out to her. I can't do anything about her not getting back to me, and I could kick myself for how this day ended. What started out as a wonderful evening crashed and burned pretty darn quickly, and I only have one person to blame: me.

CHAPTER TWENTY-SIX
Mitch

Regina keeps giving me the strangest look today at work. I wish she would focus on the report from the last patient I brought into the ER instead of doing this non-verbal interrogation. What's worse is that Jolene is working today, and that means even more questions. Jo has her ear to the ground when it comes to dirt on anyone. If I didn't know any better, I would think she worked for the Jacksons as a spy.

"Last night was fun," Regina says. "You skipped out before Liza got sloppy drunk."

"It wouldn't be moon bathing without *that* happening."

"So..." Regina taps on the counter with her pen. "Where did you take off to?" She waggles her eyebrows like she already knows the answer.

I pinch her nose. "You're so nosy. Why should I tell you anything?"

"Because we're practically related and because..." Regina looks around before speaking again. "Because you like her. Admit it."

"It doesn't matter."

"Just so you know, I don't buy her journalism line one stinking bit. After Jackie came in for her reaction, Jolene let it slip that Jackie's insurance was the same as ours. Imagine that."

A deep sigh escapes my lips. "Jo is going to get us into a lot of trouble with her loose lips."

Regina scrunches up her brow. "What do you mean?"

"She's a—"

"Mitch, I was hoping I would run into you today."

Regina and I lock eyes as Jackie walks up to us. She's dressed in a blue business suit, and her hair is up in a bun, but her expression is a combination of frazzled and scared. She hardly even resembles the person I was tongue wrestling with last night.

"Hey, Jackie." Regina stands up from her seat at the nurses' station. She turns over the paper she's working on and adds, "Still working on your *story*?"

With a flat smile, Jackie says, "Yes. I'm almost done. Er, Mitch, can I speak to you in private?"

"Would you like to shadow me today to see the glamorous life of an ER nurse?"

Jackie's eyes ping pong back and forth between me and Regina. "That would be great. But first, can I steal Mitch from you for just a moment? This can't wait."

Regina stares at me with mischief in her eyes as she replies to Jackie. "Sure. The break room is down the hall to the left, or if you want more privacy, the supply closet is on the right. But truth be told, that's so cliché."

Jackie's face blanches, but she recovers in a flash. "I wouldn't do this if it wasn't important... for my story."

Uh-oh.

She follows me down the hallway to the break room. I pick up the newspaper that someone left lying out and pretend to read the headline story. "We've already gone over this. We're cool."

She snatches the paper out of my hand and folds it. "I need to talk to you. It's really important."

"Is this about your 'story'?" I ask, using air quotes.

"Yes, and you're the only one that can clear something up with me."

I close the door and lean up against it. "What's going on? And how am I the one that can help?"

Jackie paces through the break room, her hands shake so much that she squeezes them into fists. She throws her shoulders back, and I can only imagine this is what she's like when she's speaking to someone on the witness stand, if that's the kind of lawyer she is. "Late spring or early summer. Pickle festival. Dr. Melanie Ballard."

I shut my eyes and pray I don't rat myself out. After downing my shot, I say, "Can you be more specific?"

Jackie crosses her arms. "First, tell me about Melanie Ballard, otherwise known to those around here as Doc Mel."

I would rather stick needles under my fingernails than talk about Mel with Jackie. It's like ripping off the scab of a wound that was so close to being healed. I clear my throat and say, "Mel is Gunnar's cousin. She used to be a doctor in the ER but is now with Doctors Without Borders."

"And that's all?"

"Well, we grew up in the same town, went to school together, stuff like that."

Jackie nods. "Stuff like that. Is that all?"

"What are you asking? Mel might have left without a notice, but she's a fine doctor. Everyone in this town can attest to that."

She crosses her arms over her chest and cocks her head to the side. "Do you love her?"

"No," I say, and it's one hundred percent true. "I did have feelings for her at one point, but it was just an infatuation and completely one-sided."

"Hmm."

"Jackie, just spit out what you're asking, or I'm going to have to ask you to leave."

She takes a deep breath, squeezes her eyes shut, and blurts out, "Did Dr. Ballard ask you to do anything outside of your scope of practice during the pickle festival?"

Jackie's words pin me to the back of the door. When Mel asked me to fill in for Regina while she and Clint competed in the pickle festival,

I didn't think anyone would ever find out I may have done a few tasks I shouldn't have. "I can explain."

Jackie starts up her pacing the room again. "You don't have to. Oh, Mitch, this is bad. Not only could this get you and Dr. Ballard fired, but it could be the straw that allows this hospital to be shut down." At this point, she's yelling in a stage-whisper kind of voice.

Shaking my head so hard, my brain hurts, I say, "Listen. Mel doesn't work at the hospital anymore. I questioned her orders, and she said she trusted me. Plus, no one got hurt." I throw my hands in the air as I stare at the ceiling. "How did this even show up in your findings?"

"Dr. Ballard wrote about it in her resignation letter and asked that you not be reprimanded and that she took full responsibility. But that's not how things work. Actions have consequences."

"Then fire me right now, but don't let the hospital suffer."

"That is not part of my job description. I just make recommendations." A tear slides down her cheek, but she swipes it away quickly. "Mitch, I don't know what to do."

I shrug. "Why not?"

She walks up to me and takes both my hands in hers, and after a conversation with herself, she takes a deep breath and gazes into my eyes. "Because I think I'm in love with you."

In dead silence, I try to process her words. My mouth is bone dry, and it gapes open like a dead fish's.

"Say something, Mitch."

"I—"

The door opens, and I'm jolted back into reality. Regina pops her head into the room. "Jackie, you ready?"

Jackie stiffens her spine, wipes a stray tear from her eye, and paints on a fake smile I'm sure she uses every day in her cut-throat job. "Yep. Inspire me to switch careers." Over her shoulder, she mumbles to me, "We'll talk tonight... at your apartment?"

I nod because my vocal cords are paralyzed.

And they're off, leaving me more confused than I was yesterday or the day before.

CHAPTER TWENTY-SEVEN
Jackie

My mind is even more frazzled after my profession of love to Mitch. And having to shadow Regina couldn't have happened on a worse day.

"And this is our Pyxis machine where we dispense all of our medications *after* we have an order written by the physician, of course."

She taps in a code on the keypad and touches the screen a few times. The machine makes a grinding motion, then a door pops open. Regina scoops the medication out of the drawer. "Now follow me, and I'll show you how we make sure we dispense it to the right patient. There are five 'rights' of medication administration: right patient, right drug, right dose, right route, right time. A lot of responsibility goes along with giving meds."

She sanitizes her hands, and I follow suit. "Miss Ledbetter, this is Miss Jackie. She's doing an article about Smithville and would like to watch me work. Is that okay with you?"

The little old lady perks up, but winces at her movement. "Why, yes. You have such beautiful hair. My granddaughter has hair like yours. Takes after her daddy."

Regina pats her arm. "Just relax. I'm going to give you something for the pain and another pill to get you drowsy. But first, I need to check your blood pressure." Regina checks Mrs. Ledbetter's armband, scans it to make sure she's the right patient, then performs vitals. After the lady takes the medication, Regina documents it in the computerized medical record. She then adds the blood pressure, temperature, respiration, and pulse.

She scrunches up her brow. "Mrs. Ledbetter, what's going on with your mouth?"

"It's nothing but a toothache. Since Dr. Kreth moved his practice to Moultrie, I haven't been able to see a dentist. He was the only one that would see me without charging an arm and a leg."

Regina types another note. "Don't you worry about that. We'll figure something out. You just relax, and the doctor will be in shortly."

As we leave, Regina tsks. "Poor thing. From the smell of her mouth, I'd say she has a rotten tooth, and then she fell and broke her hip. She's such a sweet thing. Sang in the choir at my father's church for as long as I can remember. She also makes the best chess pie you've ever eaten."

"She seems very kind."

"Yeah. She's genuine too."

We're walking down the hallway to the next bay when, suddenly, Regina stops and stares at me. "It's just been hard on Mitch to make lasting attachments because of his upbringing." She grins. "Silas was always confident in everything he did. Clint tried to outrun his past, but that didn't last. And Mitch was the shy, sweet one, just trying to blend into the background."

"No way he can blend now."

"That's for sure. Come on. Want to watch me clear out an impacted colon?" she asks with a smile on her face. That is a superhero.

If I learn only one thing from this experience, it's that I'm not cut out to be a nurse. Regina is amazing. Her knowledge combined with her skill and bedside manner can't be topped at any level-one trauma center.

"You know major hospitals would pay you double the money you're making now for your expertise and skill."

She shrugs like she knows it. "It's not about the money. I love this place. If you stay here long enough, you'll see that for yourself."

I already do.

I DRUM MY FINGERS ON the counter of In a Jam while I swallow my sweet tea. Mitch will be here any minute now, and I'm terrified I scared him off. I also do not know how to handle the "scope of practice" issue without messing everything up completely.

"Something on your mind?" Andie refills my tea glass then wipes down the counter. "We are non-judgmental here."

Mrs. Cavanaugh nods without looking up from the stove. "Everybody's got skeletons in their closet."

"I know what it's like to have battles with yourself over decisions. It will eat you up inside if you let it." Andie slings the towel over her shoulder then sits next to me at the counter.

"Do you know why I'm here?"

Andie smiles. "I know why you say you're here."

I cover my face with my hands. "I'm not a reporter. I'm not writing an article. I'm here to shut down the hospital." Flopping my head down on the counter, I let out a groan. "Worst person on the planet."

"I wouldn't say that." Mrs. Cavanaugh stirs the contents of a huge pot that's on the stove. "Your inner conflict means you don't want to do it, so there's that."

Andie nudges me with her shoulder. "Why would you want to shut it down?"

She sits quietly while I ramble on about my job and what I was supposed to do when I got here. And she doesn't make fun of me when I tell her how much Mitch means to me. In fact, she clutches her chest and does the cutest "aw" as I go into a little more detail than I should.

My eyes drift to the counter as I fidget with a napkin. "There is one more thing."

"You're married." Mrs. Cavanaugh makes me laugh.

"No. Definitely not married."

Andie takes the napkin away from me. "Go on."

"If I can make the case that Smithville Regional Hospital should be shut down—and I have very good evidence that it should—I..." I cover my eyes because I don't dare watch her reaction. "I'll be promoted to vice president."

Mrs. Cavanaugh whistles. "That's a huge carrot on a stick."

"Tell me about it."

"I had a big carrot on a stick when I first got here too." She motions toward Mrs. Cavanaugh. "She was here and didn't judge me. I could have sold this building and left this whole block to fall one store at a time, and I came very close to doing it."

"What changed your mind?"

Andie stands and dances around in a circle with her arms out wide. "I fell in love. With Gunnar. With this shop. With Mrs. C. Even the biddies."

I know what she means. "How do I know I'm making the right decision?"

"When it doesn't keep you up at night." Mrs. Cavanaugh takes the pot off the stove, arranges jam jars on the counter, then wipes the rim of each jar.

"I love my job, but I love it here too."

"You could live in Atlanta during the week and live here on weekends."

I snort. "Yeah, like anyone on the hospital staff would welcome me here after I put them out of jobs."

"Do you have to?" Andie asks as she pulls out the funnel and places it in the first jam jar.

"I can't cover it up. The best I can do is downplay it."

"Enough about work. What are you going to do about Mitch?"

"That keeps me up at night, too, but in a good way."

Mrs. Cavanaugh taps the funnel before moving it to the next jar. "Looks like you took my advice and kissed him."

Heat flames up my neck, and I couldn't deny it even if I wanted to. "Yes, I did. And I might have told him..."

Andie gasps and gives me a side hug. "I knew it."

"How did he take it?" Mrs. Cavanaugh screws on the lids.

"We got interrupted before he had a chance to respond. That's why I'm here."

"This should be fun."

That's what I'm hoping for.

My phone rings, jolting me out of my thoughts. When I see the caller is Melanie Ballard, my heart rate doubles in speed.

"I need to take this." I answer the phone as I leave the shop. "Hello?"

"This is Dr. Ballard," a twangy voice says over the phone. "Sorry I didn't call earlier. My time zone is way different than yours. What can I help you with?"

The moment of truth. I need to get her side of the story, even if I don't want to hear it. As I walk down the sidewalk and find a park bench to sit on, I collect my thoughts. After a deep breath, I lay out all the facts I have uncovered and wait for Dr. Ballard to give me any more information.

"Listen, Miss Dalton. I know it was not proper of me to give Mitch those orders, but I have already taken full responsibility for my actions. Don't take it out on him—or the hospital. Neither had any control over the matter."

Before I can talk myself out of it, I blurt out, "Were you in a relationship with Mitch?"

"Absolutely not. I think he was infatuated with me, but it would never have gone anywhere. And I don't know why you're asking."

Because I'm jealous.

I open my mouth to reply to her, but she adds, "This conversation doesn't have anything to do with the hospital situation, does it?"

Busted.

"It does, and it doesn't. I'm sorry I wasted your time. I know you must be very busy."

"Mitch is a good guy. Don't play with his feelings."

"Never. I..."

"Oh. Well, in that case, just for the record, Mitch is one hundred percent available."

I watch as a teenager jogs past before I'm able to form words. "Thanks, I guess."

As she disconnects the conversation, I'm left feeling more confused about what to do. My darn heart and head are having a boxing match, and neither is going to be the victor.

CHAPTER TWENTY-EIGHT
Mitch

After hearing the *L* word from Jackie, I'm a ball of nerves. I can't do anything right. Frankie has to double-check everything I do, because I can't even take a blood pressure correctly. And when Melba Kingston lost her bladder as we were transferring her onto the gurney, it just about put me over the edge. She chatted so much about her entire medical history, which I knew by heart anyway, that we didn't hand her off in the ER until almost five thirty.

And the mess with Mel... I didn't think anyone knew about it. I wish my present self could kick my past self in the balls for not standing up to Mel. I could have said, "No, Mel. Rules are rules." But no... I had to show her I was capable of doing and being more, something she could be proud of. I knew I could do the tasks. Otherwise, I wouldn't have risked it. But it was still wrong, and I knew better. Then she had the nerve to cut and run, writing that note to clear her conscience. *Thanks, Mel. You couldn't just leave. You had to kick me in the nut sack on your way out the door.*

Running a red light to get back to the café, I dare Gunnar to pull me over. I can't wait to get out of these urine-soaked clothes and finish the conversation with Jackie. She can't just tell me she's in love with me then scoot out the door, leaving me with my mouth hanging open. No woman has ever said those words to me, and hearing them in a hospital breakroom just before the woman skedaddles away from me like she wished she could stuff the words back into her mouth was not how I was hoping I would hear them.

But she did want to meet so...

I spot Jackie sitting at the counter, chatting it up with Andie and Mrs. Cavanaugh. They sound like they're having a yee-haw time. I consider running upstairs to hide for the rest of the night.

Jackie swivels in her seat and covers her mouth. "What happened to you?"

"Work happened. I know I stink. I'll just be a moment." I take two steps toward the door, and she jumps off the stool.

"I'll come with you."

I freeze, then I turn around and stare down at my pants. "I need to take a shower."

Jackie shrugs, and Mrs. Cavanaugh snorts. Andie swats at Mrs. Cavanaugh's arm. I want to crawl under the counter.

She grins. "What I mean is I can wait upstairs just as good as I can wait down here. I won't bite."

"That's a shame." Mrs. Cavanaugh clucks her teeth.

In an attempt to get out of this embarrassing situation as quickly as possible, I snatch Jackie's arm and lead her upstairs. When I close the door behind us, I point to the couch. "Make yourself comfortable. I'll be quick."

"Take your time. We have a lot to discuss."

I can't make my feet move while I watch her. She pulls out the pins in her hair and lets it fall around her shoulders, then she peels out of her business blazer and places it on the coffee table. One by one, her high heels plunk to the floor, changing her stature greatly. I wonder if this is how she usually unwinds after a hard day at work, because it's as sexy as hell.

She stretches her back. "Today, I learned I am *not* cut out to be a nurse. I don't know how they do it. You, too, by the way. It's way too much pressure."

"You get used to it."

"Mrs. Cavanaugh told me that Andie is very wealthy. She sure doesn't act like a rich person. In fact, she blushed when Mrs. Cavanaugh mentioned it."

"She inherited her grandmother's lottery winnings but has given most of it away. She's good people."

"I see that."

"Andie has done a lot to help this community thrive. I'd hate for all that work to go to waste."

"Me too."

Even I can tell she's stalling. Jackie is probably trying to decide an exit strategy from this town and her confession.

Finally able to make my legs move, I hitch my thumb over my shoulder and say, "Be right back."

"I'll be here." Her green complexion tells me all I need to know. This is the end before it even got started. I might as well just sit here and let her tell me the bad news now and not waste the hot water, but I already smell rank. She may be saying goodbye, but the least I can do is hold my head up high and take it like a man... and smell like one too.

CHAPTER TWENTY-NINE
Jackie

Mitch enters his living room, shower fresh and looking good enough to eat. He passes me with eyes trained on the floor, heads to the kitchen, and pulls out a beer. "You want one?"

"No thanks."

After a long swig, he places the bottle down on the end table. "So... what do you want to talk about? The hospital? My major screw-up? Or let's just cut to the chase and discuss your truth bomb you spilled earlier today." He clears his throat. "I think there's a five-hour rule in situations like this. You know... in case you want to revoke your words."

I take a step toward him. "No take-backs. I'm ninety-nine percent sure of my words."

He cocks his head to the side. "What about the last one percent?"

With a shrug, I say, "Waiting on your response to—"

Mitch grabs me by the waist and pulls me into him, smothering my face with kisses. With his head buried in my hair, he mumbles, "Are you sure?"

Since words don't seem to convince him, I unfasten the first button on my blouse. He swats my hands away to handle the job on his own. A button from my blouse pops loose and flies across the room in Mitch's haste to remove all of my clothing in a hurry. His lips crash back into mine, stopping only briefly as I scramble to drag his shirt over his head.

"Sorry about your blouse." His voice is all raspy.

"Don't mention it," I reply as I dive back in.

Mitch picks me up and carries me to his bed. When he places me down, I shimmy out of my skirt then help him slide off his gym shorts.

A near-naked Mitch is something to behold, and I immediately cover my less-than-amazing body with a pillow. Where his abs are rock solid, my stomach is soft and round from too many fancy corporate lunches and not enough crunches. His chest is perfectly sculpted, but mine will be saggy once my bra is removed.

His face turns stormy. "What's wrong?"

I gesture my hand in front of his body, then mine. "One of us has obviously taken better care of their body than the other."

Mitch's mouth twitches. "All I see is sheer perfection." He crawls toward me and when the heat from his skin touches mine, my body-shaming goes out the window. He yanks the pillow away from me as he reduces the distance between our bodies.

"There's so much more we need to cover."

"Later." He kisses my neck.

I clear my head and say, "But I do need to apologize for something I said when we first met."

Stopping, he leans on his elbow and stares down at me while he draws circles on my stomach with his index finger, sending an amazing tingly sensation through my body. "Go on."

"Remember that dig I made about your big truck?"

He scrunches up his brow. "I'm not following you."

My eyes trail down his body then back up. "You're definitely *not* overcompensating."

He buries his face in the crook of my neck as his body trembles with laughter. "Good to know I won't be a disappointment."

Hell, no.

"If we are doing confessionals, I guess I have one of my own."

If he tells me another problem with the hospital—or worse, if he comes clean about his affection toward Mel—I may cry or throw up. My conversation with her put me at ease, and surely, she wouldn't lie about that.

Nose to nose with me, he gazes into my eyes. His mouth twitches. "When we were fishing, I may have taken off my shirt just to impress you."

I tickle his side until he pins my hands over my head. "As if you needed to."

"Why do you think you love me? We've known each other one week. One. How is that possible that you love me?"

I sit up on my elbows and stare into his gorgeous blue eyes. There isn't one single thing not to love. "The first time I laid eyes on you, I knew you were the one, and I was either going to fall in love with you or want to kill you. Trust me, I really don't want to kill you."

He kisses my neck, leaving a trail of goose bumps in his wake. "But you're leaving soon."

"I know. Don't remind me."

Mitch groans. "Jackie, what are we doing?"

I let out a sigh. "For once, just once, I want to act on impulse and not think about how this is going to impact me in five years or how will this advance my career."

"How *will* this advance your career?"

"Ha. It will probably derail it, but I don't really care. My father will be furious, but he'll have to get over it. I do need to tell you something."

"Mm-hmm." He snuggles into my neck. When he kisses my earlobe, my brain short-circuits, and I forget all about hospitals and promotions.

"I don't want to leave," I mumble to myself.

"Then don't go back," he says as he slides on top of me. "In fact, you never have to leave this room."

That is a five-year plan I can get behind.

MITCH'S SOFT BREATHS tickle my neck as he sleeps next to me. I never want to leave the cocoon of his arms in this tiny apartment within this quaint town. I never realized how suffocating my life was until I came down here and was able to breathe. Here, there are no expectations for me to "better myself" or climb the ladder. Whatever pressure I have on myself here is put there by me, and I love the freedom.

He rolls over and snakes his arm around my waist, tugging me toward him. My hand slides up and down his forearm, landing on the top of his hand. He lets out a satisfied sigh and cups his hand over mine.

After a moment of silence, he clears his throat. "During the pickle festival, we were short-staffed in the ER. Mel, Dr. Ballard, asked me to help out, so I did. I questioned a few of her orders, but she said she trusted me. With her supervision, I did as she instructed, even though I knew I shouldn't have. No harm was done, and I didn't think anyone was the wiser."

His story so far coincides with what Dr. Ballard told me earlier. "An audit found your signature on the procedures."

"Of course it did."

A tiny bit of the green monster creeps in, and I have to ask. "If it had been anyone else other than Dr. Ballard, would you have—"

"I don't know."

"What *do* you know?"

He lets out a deep breath, swiping a stray hair behind my ear. "I know that I never loved her. I thought I did at one point, but she never gave a hang about me. It's all water under the bridge now, and I'm glad things turned out the way they did."

I hold up his hand that still covers mine and kiss his. "Me too."

"Aren't you sleepy?"

I snicker. "Quite the contrary. I think you energize me."

"In that case..." He flips me over and peppers my neck with kisses.

"Yes, please."

Mitch transforms from cute and sleepy to a hungry, determined man in less than a minute. It's hard to imagine both can be parts of the same human, a man who wants me, of all people.

HOURS LATER, AS A SMALL slice of sun peeks into the window, my phone chirps.

He whimpers. "Your phone has been going off constantly for the last hour." He yawns and stretches his arms over his head. "It must be important."

And like a crashing wave, the situation with Mitch and the hospital comes soaring back into my brain. I slide away from under Mitch's arm and out of his bed and slip on his T-shirt. I grab my cell phone and race into the bathroom to check my messages.

"I have to pee. Be right back."

There is one email from Matthew marked "urgent" and at least ten text messages from Brett, along with several from Penny. This. Is. Not. Good.

Matthew's email, sent to me but copied to everyone in the department, sends a shock wave through me. "Would you like to explain why you're dawdling onsite when the data about your hospital is evident?"

Shit.

Brett's text messages have me wanting to throw up.

Brett: *Did you see Matthew's email? Get your butt back to ATL STAT! I am back and Penny and I are trying to cover for you, but we can't hold off the boss man for much longer.*

A knock to the bathroom door sends my phone sailing into the toilet.

"Jackie, everything okay?"

"No. I, uh... Do you have any rice?"

He opens the door and grimaces. "Oh, dear. I'll go downstairs to see if Andie has any in the shop."

His footsteps get fainter, then I hear the thud of his feet on the steps. I'm going to lose the promotion and possibly lose my job, as well as with Mitch. Then the entire hospital staff is going to be uprooted. Nothing good is going to come from this.

While I wait for Mitch to return, I do my best to dry out my phone. It comes on, but flickers, and I let out a whimper. I scurry around the small apartment to retrieve my clothes and pinch my side as I zip my skirt too fast. While I hobble on one foot in an attempt to put on my heels, Mitch shows up with a five-pound bag of rice.

"I scored."

He tears open the bag, and I toss the phone into it, covering it completely with rice.

"Going somewhere?"

"Yeah, I have a lot of work to do today."

He must mistake my lack of eye contact to mean that I'm leaving out some important details, because he takes my chin in his hand and tips my head up. "Why are you leaving in such a hurry? You don't want to do the walk of shame, do you?"

"Nonsense. And is that a thing in a small town?"

He chuckles. "It's worse. And just so you know, Mrs. Cavanaugh is already downstairs, working her breakfast magic."

"Shoot."

"She's cool." Mitch scratches his head then lets out a breath. "I know those emails were probably from work, but can you spare a few minutes to have breakfast with me?"

The chest constricting thing starts up again. "I don't know."

"What are you hungry for?"

I take a step backward and scan his half-dressed body. "I'm definitely not a vegetarian."

He throws his head back and belts out a laugh. "Oh, Myers, don't tease me. And I thought you had a nut allergy."

"Always the comedian."

He grins. "Come on. Ten minutes, tops."

I do my best to slow my breaths. It's hard enough to breathe, let alone eat. But his sweet eyes beg me to stay a little longer. What's done is done. Whether I eat breakfast or not, it's not going to change the outcome. I resign myself to the fact that Matthew is not going to be happy with me now or fifteen minutes from now.

Spying Mitch's baseball cap, I snag it and place it on my head. "Why not? Let's eat."

He laughs as he wags his head. "I guess that's yours now, huh?"

I slide it into my purse and grin as we descend the steps. He could be talking about the hat or his heart. I'm hoping it's both.

CHAPTER THIRTY
Mitch

Hand in hand, we take the stairs from my apartment in search of whatever deliciousness Mrs. Cavanaugh is cooking up.

She waves then continues kneading a batch of dough. "Morning, Miss Jackie, Mr. Mitch."

"Hey," I say, feeling like I got caught stealing cookies from a cookie jar. I bet I have a neon sign over my head that reads "Got laid last night... and this morning."

"Something tells me you might be extra hungry this morning."

Yep. Big. Neon. Sign.

We settle into stools at the counter as Mrs. Cavanaugh pours us piping-hot cups of coffee.

After one sip, Jackie lets out a moan of satisfaction. She really shouldn't do that. "Mrs. Cavanaugh, if you ever get tired of Smithville, you'd be an amazing barista in Atlanta."

I don't want to think about Jackie leaving right now, and the way she mentions it so casually burns a hole in my heart.

"Pfft. This is my home, born and raised. I got everything I need right here: friends, family, fresh air, and lots of eye candy."

I choke on my coffee. As I cough, Jackie pats me on the back.

"Child, I told you to climb that tree, didn't I?"

Sweat trickles down my back as I relive every moment of last night. It's etched into my memory and will go down as one for the books.

"You're smiling." Mrs. Cavanaugh points a spatula at me.

I snap to attention. "Was I?"

"Mm-hmm." She slides two plates of biscuits and gravy in front of us. "You need your energy if you're going to have any sort of afternoon delight later on."

My eyebrows rise, and I don't know how to reply to her. Forget the part about her being a barista. She should be a trial attorney. I bet she would be a force to be reckoned with in the courtroom, with her wit and zingers.

Andie stumbles in, her hair in a messy bun. "Sorry I'm late. Gunnar has to pull a double shift today, so we only had a little bit of time to..."

I hold out my hand for her to stop. "We get it. No details needed."

She flings on an apron and assists Mrs. Cavanaugh with the baking. "What's up with the bag of rice?"

Jackie slides her phone out of the bag and presses the power button. It comes to life. "A water emergency, but looks like it's working now. I do owe you a bag of rice."

"Nonsense. Glad it turned out okay."

Jackie's phone pings again, and she lets out a groan.

I whisper in her ear, "Is it... you know who?"

She nods. "It's okay. I spilled the beans to Andie and Mrs. Cavanaugh yesterday. They know I'm not a reporter."

I let out a sigh of relief. I hate keeping secrets from my family. Maybe one by one, they'll know everything and won't judge her for what she thought she had to do.

Jackie's brow furrows. "Ugh. I know Brett's trying to help, but now he's saying he may have to do my dirty work for me."

The selfish side of me wants to tell her to let him. That way, he'll be the bad guy. But I stay silent. Jackie rubs her temples as her thumbs fly over her phone screen.

Andie refills our coffee cups. "But if he tells your boss or does the 'dirty work,' won't he get the VP position?"

Jackie's face blanches as she stares at Andie.

A few missing pieces click into place in my head. I cock my head to the side. "Say that again?"

Andie gasps and covers her mouth with her hand. "Oh, sweet baby Jesus. Jackie, I'm so sorry. I thought Mitch knew."

"Knew what?" My jaw flexes with every word.

Jackie's hands shake so much, her phone tumbles to the floor. She squeezes her eyes shut. A sinking pit in my stomach makes me want to throw up, because I think I've been lied to all this time.

In a cold, mechanical voice, I say, "Jackie, what are you talking about?"

She opens her eyes and takes a deep breath. "This assignment was an opportunity to get promoted to vice president of SHA."

It takes a moment for everything to register, and I just stare at her like a bump on a log. This has got to be a cruel joke. Finally, I give her a slow head wag and stand up.

She latches on to my arm, but I jerk it out of her reach. "But that was before I talked to Dr. Ballard, and she—"

I hold out my hands and, through gritted teeth, say, "You did what?"

Her mouth drops open at my spot-on accusation, but then she swallows and takes a deep breath. "I needed to verify with her that you weren't leaving out any important information."

I shake my head. "You couldn't trust me. Is that what you're saying? Just admit it that you used me to get the promotion. And you went behind my back when I clearly gave you the full story."

"Wait a second. Weren't *you* using *me* to keep the hospital open?"

"That's not the same, and I see you didn't deny your motives for calling Mel."

"I had various reasons for calling her, and yes, one was to confirm the incident."

"Well, I hope you got what you wanted."

She throws her shoulders back and stands tall. "I did, or at least I thought so."

Andie grimaces while Mrs. Cavanaugh busies herself at the stove. I'm so glad the Jackson sisters aren't around. That would be just the icing on this horrible cake.

"Fishing, dinner with your family, moon bathing... It was all just an act."

I stalk closer to her and, through rapid breaths, say, "I saved your life."

She has the nerve to snort. "After you served me a pie with nuts."

"And if I hadn't been at the fair *and* if the hospital had been more than five minutes away, you would have died because your EpiPen didn't work. When Marlo was in distress while in labor with Chloe... they both could have died if the closest hospital was an hour away. Every member of this community has benefited from having a local hospital, but if numbers mean more to you than humans, if your precious corner office is more valuable than everyday, hardworking people, then I pegged you correctly from the get-go. You're a heartless ambulance chaser."

She gasps, but I'm not done. I'm just getting warmed up.

I gesture to the door. "The next time you talk to Mel, tell her I don't appreciate being thrown under the bus." I snort. "You're two peas in a pod. You go do what you do best: serve yourself. I'll be over here, sleeping with a clean conscience, taking care of people who are the heart and soul of this town."

I fish in my pocket to retrieve some money and slam it on the counter, making Jackie jump. When I stomp out of the shop, I run smack dab into Regina and Clint coming into the shop.

"Bro, where's the fire?"

"Leave me alone." I walk backward and throw my hands in the air. "I screwed up big time." When he takes a step toward me, I wave him off. "Just don't. Not now."

I collapse into my truck and rest my head on the steering wheel, doing my best to get my breathing under control. I can't believe I got played like a fiddle, but not anymore. I'm done. I have a job to do—while I'm still employed, that is.

CHAPTER THIRTY-ONE
Jackie

My throat closed up when Mitch stormed out of the café. I've hurt him to the core, and I don't think there's anything I can do to recover from this.

"Mitch, wait." I grab my phone off the floor, sling my purse over my shoulder, and rush out the door to chase him down. A wall of muscle halts my forward trajectory, and Clint grabs my elbow before I fall on my butt.

"Whoa. What's going on?"

Through a cascade of tears, I say, "I have to talk to him."

Regina grimaces. "I wouldn't do that right now."

"I have to try." I run down the sidewalk just as Mitch's truck peels onto the road. My shoulders slump, and the contents of my stomach turn into a pile of acid. It's no use, so I walk back toward the inn, wiping tears that just won't stop appearing.

Halfway to the inn, I pull out my phone and call my sister. She answers on the first ring.

"Hey, little sister. How's it going?"

Through a major crying jag, I say, "I... I... messed..." My breath hitches every time I try to speak. I lean against a brick wall and take a few deep breaths in an attempt to prevent hyperventilation.

"Jackie, what happened?"

I give Gretta the abbreviated version and wait for her reply as the two old ladies with cell phones walk past. They can take as many pictures as they want. I won't be here for much longer anyway. Maybe they can blow them up, and the staff at the hospital can throw darts at my face.

"Sweetheart, what did you expect would happen? That you two would settle down there, sit on a front porch, watching the lightning bugs at night, and live happily ever after?"

Without batting an eye, I say, "Yes. In a nutshell, that's exactly what I wanted to happen. Maybe not at first, but now, absolutely, that's what I would have been happy with."

I walk the last block to the inn, which seems to take forever to appear through my tear-streaked vision. I run up the steps to my room, change into some ratty clothes, and pack my bags. Then I flop down on the floor and bury my head in my hands.

After an eternity, I stand up, wipe my face with my T-shirt, and head out in search of fresh air and one last hurrah before I leave. I've ruined everything. Mitch knew some of why I came here, so maybe he would have been understanding if I'd been honest about everything right from the start. But the hurt in his eyes, knowing I left out a huge part of the story, cut me to the core. I've ruined everything that could have been between us.

I walk down the sidewalk, the same one I traveled the first day I was in town. All the quaint shops cry out to me as if I've betrayed them too.

A G-Wagon drives past me then screeches to a halt. Regina sticks her head out the passenger-side window and says, "Jackie, we've been looking for you."

"Why?"

She climbs out of the vehicle and walks toward me as if she's afraid I'll skitter away. "Are you okay?"

"Nope," I say through my sniffles. "I ruined everything."

Regina touches my arm, and she softens her tone. "Come with me."

She leads me into the G-Wagon, and Clint drives in silence. The homes we pass are a blur, and there is no way I could find my way back to the inn on my own. Nothing looks familiar.

My breath hitches as I say, "Are you going to take me to the county line and make me walk back to town?"

Clint chuckles. "No. We're just going to talk."

He drives until I realize he is pulling into Gunnar and Andie's driveway.

"What are we doing here?"

"Mitch isn't here, if that's what you're thinking. We only want to hear your side of the story."

Regina and Clint lead me up the steps to the gorgeous log cabin, and when Andie opens the door, I fall into her arms and sob.

"I thought you were at your shop."

Andie holds me tighter. "I had more important matters to tend to."

"What am I going to do?" My words are muffled in her T-shirt.

"Shh, let's get this sorted." Andie pulls me into the house, and we sit at a massive bar in her kitchen. "Gunnar isn't here, so it's just us gals." She stares at Clint, and he scoots backward out of the kitchen.

"See ya."

I let out a huge breath and tell Andie and Regina my sordid tale, and they listen without throwing anything at me, which is a major victory in and of itself, because I don't think Regina likes me very much to begin with.

Regina drums her fingers on the granite countertop. "What was the real purpose for your visit here?"

"I know it looks bad, but it started out as an easy way to get a promotion. I'd come here, find a few infractions under the guise that I was writing an article, and head back to the big city with a secured VP position. But every second I spent with him pulled me farther and farther from my life in Atlanta. I love my job, but I want a family too. It's hard to climb the ladder and have a fulfilling home life, though. And every time I've been around Chloe..." I burst into tears again as I finish my confession. "I want that. I want that with Mitch. I realize it's not logical to fall in love with someone after only one week, but I didn't. I fell in love with Mitchell Sorrow the second I met him, and I know with one hundred percent certainty that my life will never be the same."

"Why did you call Mel?"

"I was just doing my job. I needed her side of the story, but really, I wanted to make sure she didn't have a thing for Mitch too."

Regina groans. "You could have saved yourself a lot of trouble by bringing your green monster to me or anyone else in town. There was never going to be anything between them."

I cover my face with my hands. "I know that now, but I was just so darn insecure. Why wouldn't she want Mitch? I mean, have you looked at him lately?"

Andie chuckles. "If it isn't meant to be, you can't force two people to be a couple."

After a long, uncomfortable patch of silence filled with only my sniffles, Andie clears her throat. "No matter what, we're still here for you. Always."

Regina agrees.

"I didn't get the impression you liked me much."

She waves me off. "Girl, I'm always skeptical of newcomers. Just ask Andie."

"It's true."

Regina holds out a hand, and Andie puts her hand on top, then I do the same.

"Woo! Girl's rock." Andie is so cute.

"We are here if you need anything. You have a family here even if you don't ever visit Smithville again. There's something about this town that seeps into your heart and doesn't let you go."

These two girls have taken me in and treated me like one of their own when they didn't have to. They wormed their way into my heart. It's at this precise moment that I realize I've found my home... and my family. I just need to figure out a way to win back my man.

CHAPTER THIRTY-TWO
Mitch

I sit outside the Pour House Bar and stew as I decide whether to drink myself under the table today or just sit in my truck, beating myself up. The end result is the same either way, so I might as well enjoy a good stupor. I could easily go down the rabbit hole of alcohol if I'm anything like my parents.

If I weren't so pissed, I would be hurt. I'm so angry at her for leaving out a very important piece of information. Maybe I should have assumed there was something in it for her. I could have asked, but the fact that she had to call Mel to verify my side of the story makes my blood boil. I'm even more furious at myself for lowering my guard and letting her in. Regina tried to warn me, and I didn't listen. I just dove in without considering the consequences. I should have kept my head down and focused on my job, and whatever happened with the hospital, I would deal with it like the rest of the staff. But I had to go and get my heart involved. This is much dumber than pining over my high school crush for more than a decade.

Groaning, I swing open my truck door. When I enter the bar, the loud honky-tonk music overwhelms me. Still, I find a seat at the bar and order a beer and a shot. I'm about to order a second round even before I take the first swig when a beefy hand clamps down on my shoulder. I turn to find Gunnar standing behind me.

He scowls. "You plan on driving tonight?"

"Maybe I'll get an *Uber*," I say, remembering Jackie's comment from a week ago. It infuriates me that I have that memory.

Concern etches across his face while he plunks down next to me. "I know better than anyone else on the planet what you're feeling right now. Don't let it consume you, because it will eat you alive."

Pointing my beer bottle at Gunnar, I say, "Do you realize *your* cousin left the country and the entire hospital is going to be punished for what she ordered *me* to do. I should have told her no, and I did at first, but I thought she was warming up to me, so I let it cloud my judgment. I'm so stupid."

As I get Gunnar up to speed about the hospital and Jackie's promotion, he grimaces. "I'm sorry. There's not much more I can say about that. Let's get out of here. The gym is still open. We can sling iron. It will make you feel better."

"Not in the mood. Besides, you're on duty."

He grabs me by the collar, reminding me how strong he is. "It wouldn't be the first time I took my break to get in a few sets. Let's go." Gunnar drags me out of the bar and toward my truck. "I'll drive."

I shrug out of his grip. "I'm not drunk. You got here too quick for that to happen. I didn't even down the first shot, thanks to you."

He backs away and holds up his hands. "Okay, but you better drive the speed limit, and I'm going to be right behind you... all the way to Silas's house."

"I don't live there anymore."

Gunnar quirks up an eyebrow. "Do I have to arrest you?" He points to my truck. "Drive, and I'll meet you there."

"Fine." I slam my truck door extra loudly to make sure he knows how ticked off I am.

I drive as instructed, and Gunnar stays right on my tail in his squad car the entire way. When I pull up to Silas's house, I see Clint's G-Wagon.

"Just great. Let the interrogation begin."

Marlo opens the door, and my family surrounds me with hugs and love. Carson and Caleb cling to my legs as I waddle into the house, doing my best not to step on any little feet.

I run a hand through my hair. "Let's get this over with. I screwed up. I'm going to lose my job, and the hospital will get shut down all because of me."

Silas lets me sit in his favorite recliner while he joins Clint and Gunnar on the couch. Marlo picks up Chloe from her bassinet and hands her to me. If there is one thing that can make the world worth living for, it's this sweet angel. Chloe coos while she bobbles around until she gets comfortable. I kiss her head and inhale her intoxicating baby scent.

Marlo sits on the coffee table in front of me and pulls her boys down to sit next to her. "We can't do anything about any of that. Whatever happens to the hospital or to your job will happen. Now, what about Jackie?"

The mention of her name makes my blood boil. "What about her? She got what she wanted. Jackie Myers Dalton is now the new VP of the Southeastern Hospital Association."

"What's *vee-pee*?" Carson asks his mother.

"Shh."

Clint replies to Carson, "It means vice president. She's not the head honcho, but next in line."

Carson turns to his brother and nods. "Kind of like Daddy."

Caleb seems to be okay with Carson's assessment, and Marlo covers her smile with her hand. "I'm going to give these two a bath, but please remember how much we love you, and I'm proud of you for putting yourself out there."

I snort. "Not that it did a lot of good."

"Come on, boys. Bath time."

"Aw, Mommy."

"Boys," Marlo commands, and they snap to attention and follow their mother down the hallway.

Gunnar leans over to watch the kids trotting down the hallway, and when the bathroom door closes behind them, he snaps back to full attention. "Okay. Spill. This isn't just about your job."

Silas, Clint, and Gunnar mean the world to me, and I know they only want to help, so I'll calm it with the attitude. I let out a sigh. "I let her in, and look what happened. I should have just stayed in my bubble and been the unattached uncle. Every family has one, right?"

"So you fell for someone. That's normal." Clint kicks my shoe. "It means you're human and alive."

"Why can't there be one decent woman left in Smithville? I had to go and 'move on' with someone who was never going to stay here to begin with. I knew that part, but her doing this, using me for a promotion..."

Silas enters the kitchen, retrieving Coke bottles for everyone.

"And she went behind my back to call Mel."

Silas lets out a low whistle as Gunnar opens his bottle and takes a swig. "I tried to not get attached to Andie, especially when I knew the whole time she was planning to leave. My heart had other ideas. Sometimes you got to take chances and hope things work out."

I take a swig from my Coke bottle. "What am I supposed to do now?"

"Talk to her," Silas says. "Mitch, my dear, sweet, baby brother. I've always worried about you. Mom left when you were so little. And then Pops did what he did... You didn't have a chance to see what a loving couple looks like."

Tears well up in my eyes, and I wipe them away before anyone sees them. *Dammit, Jackie, for turning me into a softie.* "You and Marlo seem to have it pretty much figured out."

Clint squeezes my shoulder. "And I know Regina and I are just now getting it right, but I've always loved her. You were always the reserved one, afraid to care too much."

"That's Mel's fault," Gunnar pipes in. "I love my cousin, but I think she led you on in some ways even though I honestly think she never had any intention of following through. If she hadn't left, you would have been old and gray and still chasing after her. She did you a favor when she scrammed."

"Yeah, but the first intelligent, sassy woman who breezes into town, I get the 'can't help its.' I just wished I had learned my lesson before..."

Silas jumps up, peeks down the hallway, then whispers, "My boys do not need to hear about S.E.X. yet."

"Me either." Clint shivers.

Gunnar grimaces. "Uh... did the bed break on you?"

Confused, I ask, "What?"

"I'm telling you it's old, and I—"

Clint holds out a hand to stop Gunnar. "Already took care of it. I bought a brand-new mattress and frame. I'm just glad Mitch got to christen it."

A smile stretches across my face, the first one in hours. "You have good taste in mattresses. I sleep like a baby, and that's good because I'm not going to be doing anything else on it ever again."

"Bro, no matter what happens, I know you'll be okay. You still have us."

I stare at them—two are blood relations, and the other is closer than a brother—and I know I'll be fine. Even if I'm without a job or without someone to care for, I'll be okay. Jackie will be gone by Sunday, if she's not already gone. And I'll figure out what my next steps will be. Until I get the boot from the hospital, I'll do my best to power through. That's how Sorrows roll.

"I'll be fine, eventually." I stand and hand Chloe back to her father. "Sweet girl, remember, I'm your favorite uncle."

"In your dreams." Clint gives me a hug and whispers, "Fight for what you want."

I nod, but I don't even know what I want anymore. I guess I need to figure that out before I do anything.

As I leave Silas's house, something unusual lying in the bed of my truck catches my eye. It is Jackie's foam finger wedged in under my boom box. How it didn't fly out while I was driving, I'll never understand. It just rests there, taunting me. I snatch it up and toss it inside my truck.

While driving back to In a Jam, I pass the Peach Fuzz Inn. Jackie's tiny car sits out next to the road, so I pull in behind it. I snatch up the foam finger and secure it under her windshield wiper. That's all she ever wanted from Smithville anyway.

CHAPTER THIRTY-THREE
Jackie

No amount of makeup would conceal the dark circles under my eyes. No sleep, off-and-on bouts of tears, and the occasional phone calls to Penny had me up all night. She was the one who convinced me I was in no shape to drive back to Atlanta last night and that I should probably at least try to get a good night's sleep.

No such luck.

Bobby James takes my credit card, and while the transaction processes, he smiles. "I hope you had a nice visit here."

I shrug. "Work was ugh, but everyone I met was so genuine."

He holds up a finger. "I have something for you."

Hope springs up in my heart that maybe Mitch left me a note. I would do anything to make it right between us.

"I finished this one last night and thought you might like it." Bobby James hands me a copy of *Lords of London*, which I haven't read yet, and even though I'm deeply disappointed it has nothing to do with Mitch, I'm touched to the core that he gave me his book.

I clutch the paperback to my chest before I place it in my oversized bag, right next to Mitch's baseball cap. My breath hitches. "Thank you so much."

"Have a safe trip back to Hot-lanta."

If I don't leave right now, I'll convince Bobby James to give me a long-term rental agreement so I can hide in this inn forever.

With a final wave, I exit the inn for one last stop. There was no way in Hades that I would leave town without saying goodbye to my new bestie, Andie, so I take a walk down to In a Jam. She wrote me this morning to tell me she wanted me to stop by on my way out. Mitch's truck is nowhere to be seen, so I'm fairly certain I won't run into him. He hasn't opened any of my messages and won't answer my calls, so no matter how I try to apologize, I guess he's not interested in hearing what I have to say.

When I open the door to the café and the familiar bell jingles, tears begin to well up in my eyes. This is the last time I'll see these amazing people. Mrs. Cavanaugh busies herself behind the counter, and when Andie sees me, she stops what she's doing to rush toward me. As she envelopes me in a big hug, the last of my brave armor falls to the floor with a thud.

"I wish you didn't have to go."

My breath catches in my throat. "Duty calls."

Andie's mouth turns down into a frown as she ushers me to a booth. She sits in front of me as Mrs. Cavanaugh brings me a breakfast plate.

"Thank you so much. You have been so kind to me when you didn't have to," I say to the elderly woman.

"Honey, it's what we do. God is in charge of sorting the wheat from the chaff, not us."

I look to Andie, and she translates for me. "What she means is it's not up to us to pass judgment. Lord knows, I'm the last person to criticize someone's actions."

Mrs. Cavanaugh pats my shoulder before she leaves to tend to another customer.

Andie turns to me and asks, "Have you thought about what you're going to do?"

I shrug. "I'm going to do my best to convince my boss not to close the hospital. My data, other than that one snafu, might be convincing enough. It's impossible to know what he'll do, and unfortunately, he has the last word."

She quirks up an eyebrow. "I meant what you're going to do about Mitch."

Taking a bite of my eggs, I pause to consider her words. "He won't answer my calls or texts. I can't make him talk to me."

"I figured as much." The bell over the door rings, and Andie's eyes focus on the person who made the door chime. I rotate to see Mitch standing there like a statue and as white as a ghost.

"Hey, Mitch. Did you forget something?" Mrs. Cavanaugh points to his phone sitting on the counter.

Like he has tunnel vision, he zeroes in on the phone, snatches it off the counter, and shoves it in his pocket. He turns on a dime, and just as he's about to open the door, Andie nudges my foot with hers.

"Mitch," I say in a quiet voice, causing him to freeze.

I jump up and stand near him, knowing better than to touch him. The last thing I want is for him to run away.

"I'm so sorry. I promise I'll do everything in my power to spin this to the advantage of the hospital."

He snorts as he stares at his work boots. "Spin."

"Bad choice of words."

"Just do what you need to do. I'm so looking forward to seeing how this plays out."

Chewing on my bottom lip to keep from crying, I say, "Isn't there anything I can say that won't upset you?"

He shakes his head. "I don't think so, but there are two things you can *do* for me."

Hope springs in my heart, and I step forward. "Anything."

Mitch swallows hard and pins me in my place with his gaze. "The first is to get the hell out of *my* town."

His words hit me like a slap to the face. I was leaving anyway, but this feels more like I'm being kicked out of town. I look to Andie, who nibbles on a fingernail.

He swallows hard. "And the second is... I want my hat back."

My lip quivers, and I nod as I fish out the Atlanta Braves baseball cap from my oversized bag. I stretch out my arm, and he snatches it from me, shoves it on his head, and walks out of In a Jam.

Over his shoulder, he says without any emotion, "Don't forget to have new business cards printed with your new title."

His words sting, but him wanting his hat back sucks the life out of me more than my anaphylactic reaction did. His baseball cap was the last of my hope that anything could be salvaged. There is nothing left here but a handful of memories that I'll cherish for the rest of my life.

After one last hug from Andie, I walk back to the inn, climb into my very tiny car, and set the GPS for Atlanta. The last thing I notice is the sign that reads "You're leaving Smithville. Come back soon." Then I ugly cry all the way back to Atlanta.

CURLED UP ON MY SISTER'S couch, clutching the foam finger to my chest, I recount my week, and it's the hardest thing I've ever done. Reliving every moment with Mitch and all the other colorful residents of Smithville results in using an entire box of tissues.

"What a week." Gretta sips her glass of Merlot while I sulk.

"I'm a mess, and I don't know what to do about it."

"You let it become personal. Once that happens and emotions are involved, you can't be objective. Didn't you learn anything from law school?"

I cover my face with a pillow and let out a groan. "I know, and that's exactly what I tried to avoid, but then I laid eyes on the most beautiful man I have ever seen... He could go mano a mano with me all day long."

After a bit of silence, Gretta places her wine glass down. "It's not just the job or the man. It has to be something else. What is it?"

Without missing a beat, I reply, "Chloe. I want a Chloe."

"Who in the world is Chloe?"

Just thinking of that precious infant makes my heart swell with love. "She's Mitch's baby niece who is the cutest thing."

Gretta groans. "They are all cute until they keep you awake all night and suck until your tits are raw."

I chuckle. "But aren't they worth it?"

She smiles slowly. "Yeah, most days."

I sit up on the couch and toss her the pillow. "I want that. I want it all. The diaper changing at three a.m. The puking—"

"And the raw tits."

Bopping her in the face with the foam finger, I add, "That, too, but I also want those sweet coos and the smell."

She giggles.

My thoughts go back to the first time I saw Chloe at the festival. Mitch held her in his arms and immediately went into complete "dad mode," transforming her from foul to fresh, and he didn't even bat an eye about it. "Mitch helps out, and it's not even his own child. He seems to enjoy all of it."

"Women are suckers for a handsome man carrying a baby, so maybe it's a ploy."

"Mitch isn't like that. So, I don't just want babies. I want *his* babies. I want him. I want the career and the family life."

"It's hard to have it all, but if you can figure out a way, I say go for it."

"Did I mention that he saved my life?"

"What?"

I nod. "After he almost killed me with a pie that had a pecan crust, of all things."

Gretta's eyes are as big as saucers.

"But he saved my life and wouldn't leave my side until he knew for sure I was out of danger."

Gretta stares off and blows out a breath. "Damn. No wonder you're such a mess."

Cringing, I say, "Would it be awful to not want the promotion?"

"Don't let Father hear you say that."

"I have a lot to think about before Monday's meeting, and I certainly need to figure out how to do damage control. A lot of livelihoods are on the line."

After a pointed stare, she nods. "And a few hearts."

I would be in denial if I didn't have that on the forefront of my mind and stamped across my forehead. Smithville needs that hospital, so no matter how Mitch feels about me, I have to do everything in my power to make things right for the town.

CHAPTER THIRTY-FOUR
Mitch

Even with two little hellions using me as a human jungle gym, I still can't snap out of my funk. Marlo insisted I hang with the family instead of wallowing in my pity in my tiny apartment all day. Turns out, I can do both at the same time. *Who knew?*

Silas switches channels until he lands on one of those obscure stations that show old TV shows. It beats watching reality shows where everyone finds true love, at least for the season. A commercial comes on and the actor states, "Have you or someone you love suffered anaphylaxis after ingesting nuts from an unknown source? If so, you might be eligible for compensation."

"Turn it."

He switches the channel, and a commercial for Keebler Pecan Sandies starts up. Silas chuckles and turns it again. On this channel, Elmer Fudd is hunting Bugs Bunny, and an ugly growl spews from my throat. I'll never be able to watch Looney Tunes again without thinking of *her*.

Silas turns off the television and shakes his head. "It's not meant to be, brother."

I rise. "I think I'm going to hang out at the lake today."

"Want me to come with you?"

"Naw. Stay here and enjoy your family."

I snag my baseball cap from the coffee table, and a waft of Jackie's scent enters my olfactory system as I place the cap on my head. Damn her for ruining everything, including my hat. That's sacrilege to a small-town guy. My phone beeps, and it's an email from the director at the

195

hospital. There will be an important email to be sent to all staff on Tuesday. Bile rises in my throat—I know exactly what that's going to be about. Jackie said she had a meeting on Monday, so Tuesday will probably be my last day at work.

Before I can call her, Regina texts me: *Did you see the email? Come over. Let's discuss.*

I just want to be left alone, but knowing her, she's going to bug the crap out of me until I give in, so I write her back as I drive to her apartment: *On my way.*

Waiting at the door to her apartment, she flings her arms wide when I reach her. Without asking, she wraps me in a hug, and together, we walk inside. Clint is sitting on the couch, playing a video game.

"Please take Regina's controller. She's too easy to beat."

Regina rolls her eyes and walks in front of the television, making Clint sway to the side in order to see his soldier. I slide down to sit next to Clint and start pummeling his man.

"On second thought, give it back to her."

"Ha. Too late."

"So, the email." Regina's words distract me from the game.

"What about it?" I ask as my man runs up a hill to throw a grenade.

"Do you think it's about what Jackie found?"

"Of course it is, and because you and Clint were off playing scavenger hunt, I filled in for you, so now I'm going to lose my license, along with my job. I won't even get to work anywhere else."

"That sucks, and if Mel was here right now, I'd give her a piece of my mind. But why did you administer IV medications? You knew you shouldn't have done that. She knew better."

I take a deep breath and stare at the buttons on the controller. "Because Mel was confident that I could do it. She believed in me."

Regina's pity face doesn't help my cause. "Mitch, you thought she would finally fall madly in love with you if you showed her how good you were at your job? You *are* good, and she already knew that. She took advantage of your feelings, and look where it got you. She ran away and won't be here when it all blows up in your face and when this town goes without a hospital."

"Don't you think I know that already? You don't have to beat me over the head with it. I'm an idiot." My voice cracks like a thirteen-year-old boy's, pissing me off.

"You're not an idiot," Clint barks out. "You're always trying to prove yourself with people. You think you're never good enough or that you're going to end up just like Mom and Dad. Little brother, that could not be more wrong. You're the smartest of us all. You have a big heart, and I'm sorry women take advantage of that."

I toss the controller onto the coffee table and watch it skitter onto the floor, pretty much like my hopes. "Jackie is just like Mel. She's smart, driven, career minded, *and* has an agenda." After a moment of silence, I say, "I think I'm going to join the monastery."

Regina bursts out laughing. "I think you have to be Catholic to be a monk."

"And celibate," Clint adds.

I clearly did not think this through. "Maybe you're right. Plus, I kind of like my hair the way it is too."

"Lots of women like your hair. Just saying."

Heat rises up my neck. "Shut up."

Chewing on her lip, Regina spits out, "I can't take it anymore. We ran into Jackie after you stormed out of In a Jam. I took her to Andie's to talk."

I stare at Regina like she's grown horns. "Why did you do that? Are you going to betray me too?"

"It wasn't like that, bro. We were riding down the street and saw her. It wasn't planned." Leave it to Clint to come to Regina's rescue.

Crossing my hands over my chest, I fume. "Why?"

Regina sits on the coffee table, and Clint abandons the video game. "She feels really bad about how things went down. Let's hope her meeting tomorrow won't be as bad as we fear. Perhaps she still cares for you."

"Pfft. She cares about herself. I got played like a fiddle. It's plain and simple. And her not trusting me... She had to go behind my back and talk to Mel. That was low."

"Okay. I get that, and maybe she had her reasons, but enough about that. How do *you* feel about *her*?" Regina's arched eyebrow ticks me off as much as her question.

"Nothing," I say through gritted teeth. "I feel nothing."

"I don't believe that." Regina gives me a shove on the shoulder.

"Believe what you want, but she went behind my back and talked to Mel, the one person who got me and the hospital in this mess to begin with. Plus... my past feelings for Mel... I could never forgive someone for doing something like that."

Regina groans and smacks me on the arm. "Forgiveness is easier than you think." She points to Clint and adds, "Your brother left me and even divorced me—"

"Actually, I forgot to file the paperwork, remember?"

She pins him in his place with her stare. "Stop talking." Focusing back on me, she continues. "My point is, if I can forgive Clint, then maybe you can find it in your heart to forgive Jackie. I think she's really sorry, and I'm certain she still cares about you."

I think back to Jackie's expression the last time I saw her—she looked as miserable as me. It's obvious she didn't get any sleep either and all this is eating her up inside too. But she caused all of this, so my empathy only goes so far.

"You're a hopeless romantic. If all of that is true, then why isn't she beating down the door trying to talk to me? Why didn't she call me over and over to explain? I'll tell you why. It's because she got what she wanted. It's plain and simple, so easy to understand even a simple hillbilly like myself can see it."

Regina holds her hands out in defense. "Okay, if that's the way you see it, but I think you're wrong."

"Tell me that again on Tuesday when we get canned."

She takes my hands in hers and squeezes my fists. "I'm sorry if you feel that I'm not supportive of you and am taking her side, because that's not the case at all. I just like to have faith in people. I believe things will work out the way they are supposed to, eventually."

"I'll have to let you have enough faith for the both of us, because I just can't find any."

Her phone chirps, and when she reads the message, she groans. "Uh... you might as well see this now since it will be viral by the end of the day."

I take her phone and see the title of the latest Biddy's Blog: "Nut-thing is as it seems." "I don't want to read it."

Clint takes the phone and reads it out loud. "Nut-thing is as it seems. It appears our little out-of-town guest is not a journalist after all. Who didn't see that one coming? She wasn't writing an article for *Southern Living* or *Field and Stream*, and she certainly wasn't here to write for *The Clipper, Nuts and Dried Fruit Magazine*. We don't know—yet—what she was up to, but something stinks, and we're not talking about the wild chickens prancing down Main Street. Only time will tell what that little auburn beauty, who caught the eye of our Stud, was up to. One thing is for sure—the last time she was spotted in Smithville, her eyes were puffy. No allergic reaction to blame it on this time. I guess we do that to people. Her shell is now cracked, and let's sit back to see what her next move will be. This Smithville native hopes she comes back soon."

Clint glances over at me and frowns. "Their blogs are getting weirder by the minute. Not that I read them, of course."

"Sure you don't, honey." Regina kisses his cheek. "None of us read them."

"It doesn't matter. It won't be long before everyone knows the truth anyway."

"What are you going to do?"

I turn to Clint. "I don't know. Do you think our family is cursed?"

"Nope. Our parents were selfish. They left us to fend for ourselves. You couldn't do that to anyone, not even Jackie. If she was in a car wreck on Main Street, you'd still try to save her. It's how you're wired."

My wiring gets me in trouble every time. I think it's high time to for me to get an upgrade and install a new electrical system with better insulation to avoid getting burned again.

CHAPTER THIRTY-FIVE
Jackie

My sallow skin, puffy eyes, and unkempt hair do not exude professionalism, but it is what it is. I stayed up all night working on my report, and my face shows it. I hope what I put together works, and if I can't save the hospital, I'm going to do my best to save Mitch's career.

Penny leans against the bathroom vanity as she watches me pull my hair into a tight bun. "You're not the same person you were just a week ago. You're different—better, if you don't mind me saying."

I laugh as I slide on my blazer. "I'm not different, just the person I have always been, but that part of me was buried deep. Way deep."

She smooths out her blouse and grins. "For the record, I knew that girl was down there somewhere. This business isn't for the faint-hearted, or anyone with a heart, for that matter. And you've been the only person I've worked with in the business that has a heart. In fact, if it weren't for you, I'd have left a long time ago."

My heart swells with her confession, and I could say the same about her. She's always listened to me and been my biggest cheerleader. While I'm surrounded by sharks, she's my fellow dolphin.

"You're very kind. Just remember you said that when I'm devoured in there."

"One last thing." She glances under the bathroom stalls. "Do you love him?"

My mouth turns down into a frown. "It doesn't matter."

With a sad expression, she follows me out of the bathroom and into the boardroom then whispers, "Yes. It. Does."

Brett stands in the hallway. "Can we talk?"

He's the absolute last person I want to talk to right now. "No. I have nothing to say."

Right before I enter the boardroom, he snags my arm and pulls me back. "This won't take long." He leads me to his office and closes the door.

Crossing my arms over my chest, I say, "What do you want?"

Brett scrubs his face. "I know you still think I said something to Matthew, but I didn't send him anything to him about Smithville Regional. Whatever he knows, he found out on his own."

My mouth drops open. "What are you saying?"

"I don't know exactly what he knows, but he asked me to..."

My eyebrows raise. "Go on."

"He asked me to add Smithville Regional to my presentation."

"What?"

"Shh." He peeks out his office door to see if I raised any suspicions.

We stand there, staring at each other for the longest time. I'm not sure if I believe him. He's tried to trip me up so many times, that this could be another way to mess with me.

"Are you sure it wasn't your idea?"

"I promise it wasn't. And he insisted I not tell you before the meeting, but I couldn't hold it in any longer. It wouldn't be right for you to be ambushed in front of everyone."

My head is swimming from this newfound knowledge. "Why would he do that? Does he not trust me to be objective?"

Brett runs a hand through his hair as he perches on the edge of his desk. "I don't know. I'll do my best to round out the edges of that specific issue, but I just wanted you to have a heads up and that it wasn't my idea. I want the promotion as bad as you do, maybe more, but you're my oldest friend and I would never go behind your back if he didn't force me to."

As much as Brett is a thorn in my side, he is a good guy deep down. He rarely lets it shine, but when it matters, he lets the good Brett appear.

"He already offered you the position, didn't he?"

When he doesn't reply, I have my answer. This is just great. It's like I ruined everyone's lives, including mine for absolutely no reason.

He lets out a breath. "I'm sorry."

When he exits his office, I lean back against his desk and breathe a sigh of relief. He can use all the Smithville data because I have a better idea.

I rush into the boardroom and say to Matthew. "I need Penny for five minutes."

"Why?"

"Trust me. It will be worth it."

I motion for Penny to follow me down to my office, then I slam the door behind her. "I have to start over with my project. Can you help me?"

"Absolutely."

AFTER BRETT'S EXTENSIVE report on both our hospitals, he looks a little green around the gills. But kudos to him for burying the Mitch incident so deep into his report that it barely showed up on a single slide.

Matthew smiles like a proud papa, making me want to throw up. He turns to me. "I'm sure you didn't mind. I thought it would be better if we consolidated the presentations into one."

With the best fake grin I can muster, I stand. "Of course not, but I still want to present *my* findings, as well."

He shakes his head as he checks his watch. "Not necessary."

"I think it is. While Brett's evaluation of Smithville General was quite thorough, there were a few items he would not have known about without being onsite."

Brett clears his throat. "I agree."

Thank you!

Matthew cocks an eyebrow. "You have three minutes."

Yes!

Penny adjusts my blazer and hands me the flash drive with my revised presentation on it. "You've got this."

I'm either the bravest or dumbest person on the planet.

She gives me a thumbs-up before I turn to face six scary men glaring at me. If I had a dime for every time one of them was late for a meeting because they were playing virtual golf in their offices, I would be a wealthy woman.

I slide the flash drive into the laptop and open up my presentation. "This is a little unconventional, but I think it's the best way to present the hospital I was assigned."

I take a deep breath, and one by one, I look each person in the eye. "Smithville has a population of ten thousand, four hundred and thirty-one. Actually, make that thirty-two with the newest addition, Chloe."

I click the presentation to show a picture of me holding Chloe. "She was born premature, and her mother had only minutes to get to the hospital before delivering." I click to the next photo. "This is Stanley. I watched the ER team save his life. If there hadn't been a hospital close by, knowing him, he would have toughed it out and quite possibly would have died."

Swallowing hard, I pull up a picture of Mitch standing next to his ambulance. "This is an EMT. He..." I sniffle and fight back tears. "He saved my life when my EpiPen failed to work. I don't want to think about what might have happened if the hospital wasn't just a few blocks away."

Brett grins and nods in approval.

"Ninety-five percent of Smithville Regional staff are part of the community. Those that don't live there are mainly administrative or physicians who can afford to live elsewhere. I realize the stats for this hospital's revenue are dismal, as Brett's evaluation revealed, but if we decide to eliminate this from the community, it will devastate everyone—the staff, the elderly who cannot get to another hospital..." I get choked up thinking about if Mrs. Cavanaugh needed to get to the doctor. "Closing Smithville Regional Hospital would impact every member of the community. Therefore, I recommend we allow this hospital to remain intact and discuss ways to shore up their financial situation."

I stare at each person in the room, and I can't get a good feel for how they took my suggestion, except for Brett. He actually seems pleased. Penny gives me two thumbs up, so at least I have her in my corner.

When I get the nerve to face my boss, he takes the papers in front of him and taps them on the desk to put them in order. "That was a very... interesting presentation. With your abilities, I expected more from you."

"But—"

"You took a different approach to the situation. You added a human element that cannot be quantified, and for that, I applaud your approach."

Yes!

"However, we deal with facts and figures, not feelings. Therefore, Smithville Regional will be dissolved, effective in ninety days."

"What?" My voice is so loud, Bill spills his water bottle. I never thought he would go ahead and shut it down. True, I didn't do a great job at presenting facts, but still, I showed the need for its existence.

Matthew winks. "And congratulations. You get the promotion."

"Wait. What?" My mind spins.

Brett's jaw drops. "You said..."

Matthew slowly stands and leans over the table, making Brett freeze. "I decide who gets the job, not you. Now, I have other work to do. This meeting is concluded."

Everyone in the room leaves, except Brett and me. Hand on his hips, he shakes his head. He chuckles then throws his hands in the air. "I cannot believe you got the promotion after all this."

"Me either." My brain is still spinning. Even though I went to bat for the hospital, it didn't matter. Mitch will never believe that I tried to do everything I could. "I guess it's safe to assume you're going to fill Matthew in on the part we left out, right?"

He lets out a low chuckle as he shakes his head. "No, Jackie. I won't tell. It doesn't really matter anymore anyway, right?" Then he does something that knocks the socks off me. He hugs me. "I can't believe you're my new boss, but you deserve it."

"Thanks."

I watch his retreating frame leave the boardroom, then I collapse into a chair and do my best to wrap my head around what just happened.

CHAPTER THIRTY-SIX
Mitch

I'm perched against the ER nurses' station, feeling lower than a snake's belly, when my phone chirps to announce an email. I don't have to pull it up to know the contents, and it's not going to take long before the grapevine connects all of this back to Jackie. I just don't have the strength to answer anyone's questions. After all this mess, I may get run out of town.

Not reading the email isn't going to make the situation go away, so I pull out my phone and read what I already know is going to happen.

The Southeastern Hospital Association has decided to close Smithville Regional Hospital, effective in ninety days from today. According to our revenues, our numbers have been down for three quarters in a row when most other hospitals in the region have been thriving. This was strictly a financial decision, so no specific incident led to this outcome. More details about severance pay will be forthcoming and each staff member will receive positive recommendations to assist in securing employment elsewhere. Your patients still need the same quality care as they did yesterday, so please do your best to go about your duties in a professional manner.

Sincerely, Smithville Regional Hospital Administration

I hang my head low, feeling worse than I did the day before. My problem is that I held out hope Jackie would have a 'come to Jesus' moment and change her mind, but I guess she did what she had to do. She got her promotion and left without a backward glance, leaving us in a trail of dust.

Regina races out of the break room, knocking me back into reality. "Did you read the email?"

"Yeah and why are you so happy?"

"Don't you see?"

"Yes. We are out of a job, thanks to one specific person. I see very clearly."

"No, silly. I mean, yes. That's part of it, but Jackie didn't include anything that happened with you in the report. She didn't single you out. You may think she doesn't care, but I'm telling you this one thing. She. Loves. You." She emphasizes each word with an obnoxious poke to my chest.

I roll my eyes and push past her. "She shut down the entire hospital. That's not love. That's selfish greed. End of story."

"Pfft. Oh, ye of little faith."

"You got that right. I've lost all faith in humanity. I think I've earned at least that much." I storm off down the hallway.

"Where are you going?" Regina follows me away from the emergency room.

"To find Frankie. I may not have a job for long, but I'm still on the clock today."

She runs to catch up with me then latches on to my arm. "Mitch, I need to get back to my shift, but just hear me out."

I let out an exasperated breath. "What?"

"I'm just saying not everything is as it seems. Give people the benefit of the doubt, okay? If it weren't for you, I'd still be peeved at Clint for not telling me everything. Don't be so quick to judge. Nothing good comes of it."

My head throbs, and her yapping doesn't help anything. "We just lost our jobs, and you are so perky. Don't you get it?"

She squeezes my hand and shrugs. "Sure, I get it, but I have faith we will be okay. This town will be all right. I don't know how that will look, but it will."

"Okay, Pollyanna."

"Did your entire world stop turning when your mother left?"

I recoil from her words. That is like a slap to the face for her to bring that up right now. "It felt like it."

"But it didn't. Your brothers and this community tackled it head-on, and you survived. Yes, it sucked, and it was hard. I was right there and saw it firsthand. I wouldn't wish that upon anyone, but look at you now. You never gave up, and you're not going to now. This town will rally and figure out what to do next, and we'll all find jobs somewhere. I truly believe that."

I stare off down the hallway as nurses scurry around, doing their jobs and talking softly to one another, no doubt about their pending unemployment. "I just love this place so much."

"I know you do, and so do I, but life goes on."

With a shrug, I leave the hospital and wonder how many more times I'll be able to walk the halls with colleagues, or how many more patients I'll bring in here to get the care they need. But mostly, I wonder if I did enough to make my case for the hospital or if Jackie's mind was already made up the day she rode into town. She could have called Mel from day one and been done with it, but I took a chance and let my heart open up all for nothing. She doesn't care about Smithville, and she certainly doesn't care about me. It doesn't matter that she told me she loved me, because her actions speak volumes.

I scroll past all the unread messaged Jackie sent me and send her a message. My text contains two words: *Thank you.*

There's nothing more to be said, and that was only to make myself feel a tiny bit better, because at least I can still get a job in my field. That's the only positive thing that has come out of this mess.

CHAPTER THIRTY-SEVEN
Jackie

Holding a box of my personal belongings, I stand in the entrance to my new corner office. It has floor-to-ceiling windows and a beautiful view of the city. It's everything I've always wanted. Dad was thrilled when I texted him the news, as expected. I'm still riddled with guilt that I didn't save the hospital but *still* got the promotion. I just hope I don't spend my increased income to keep me well stocked in antacids.

Penny instructs the maintenance man on where to hang my diplomas while I plunk the box on my ultra-contemporary, uber-boring executive desk and look around. My father insisted I send him a picture as soon as I got settled so he could use it as bragging rights.

"Do you need him to hang anything else?" Penny asks.

I blink out of my fog. "No. Thank you."

He leaves, and Penny cocks her head to the side. "What's on your mind?"

Flailing my arms in the air, I say, "This office. I can hear the boos from every citizen in Smithville. They're going to haunt me for the rest of my life, and I deserve it."

"You tried. I witnessed your effort. Surely that should mean something."

I shake my head. "It wasn't enough. They hate. *He* hates me." I let out a wicked chuckle and add, "I pretty much hate myself too."

Brett knocks on the doorframe. "I come bearing a gift." He holds out a peace lily plant. "Truce?" That is the nicest thing he's ever done for me.

"Jackie, I know I'm a prick on a good day."

Penny stifles a giggle.

Brett rolls his eyes. "But I'm sorry if I messed things up for you. We've known each other a long time, and I owe you so much. And you push me to excel, so without you... Well, I would be just a prick with no ambition."

Penny and I laugh as I take the plant from him. "Thank you for the plant and for your honesty, but is it so terrible that I revised what I think the definition of success looks like? There are plenty of happy and thriving people who live outside the big city. Didn't you see that in the town you were assigned?"

He shrugs. "I was in a college town, so it was mostly keg parties and study sessions, so maybe I didn't look beyond that."

"I'm glad that was your town, because I had enough of college while I was *in* college."

Brett scratches the back of his head.

Penny's eyes grow big. "Oh no. He's about to be honest with you. That's his sign. When he scratches the back of his head, he's wrestling with his feelings. Run."

Brett flushes. I think that's the first time I've ever seen him unsettled, and it's adorable how Penny can make him do that. He clears his throat. "Thank you, Penny, for ratting me out." He turns to me and sighs. "You deserve the promotion. I promise I won't be trying to undermine your every move. And she won't let me." Brett motions with his head toward Penny.

Penny winks. "You know it."

Tears well up in my eyes, and I bite the inside of my cheek to keep the tears from spilling. I've shed more tears in the last week than I have in the last ten years. My phone buzzes from inside the box, and I snatch it out. I gasp when I see Mitch sent a text.

"Everything okay?" Penny asks.

Brett steps closer, concern etches across his forehead.

With shaking hands, I open the message. *Thank you* is all it reads, but it speaks volumes. The tears won't stay in my eyes anymore. "He doesn't hate me. After all I've done, and he doesn't hate me."

"Well, duh. He loves you," Penny says.

Brett groans. "Is it from that dude? Jackie, if you don't make things right with him, you'll never forgive yourself. I know how you're wired. You're an attorney with a conscience."

I wipe the tears from my eyes and turn in circles. "What am I doing here?"

Brett and Penny stare at each other then back at me. "You're doing what everyone expects of you." She walks up to me and takes my hands in hers. "What do *you* want to do?"

As if all the gears click into place in one second, I know exactly what I need to do. I dial the one person who can help me pull this off.

When she answers, I say, "Hey, Andie, how are you?"

"Andie?" Brett turns to Penny. "I thought his name was Mitch."

Penny nudges him in the ribs and shushes him.

"I'm so sorry about what happened to the hospital. I tried to avoid that."

"From what I heard from Regina, you didn't throw Mitch under the bus. Thank you so much for doing that. I know he's been prickly lately, but he'll forgive you in time."

I lean against my desk as I put my phone on speaker. "I need to ask you a personal question. How much of your lottery money do you still have?"

"More than I can count. It's sitting in a trust right now until I finish allocating it. What's on your mind?"

Brett's eyebrows raise. "Wait, somebody in Smithville won the lottery?" All of a sudden, he's interested in the person I'm talking to.

Penny covers his mouth with her hand. "Hush."

With an evil grin on my face, I ask, "Do you want to help buy a hospital?"

Brett whistles and leaves my office. Penny high-fives me.

"Andie, are you still there?"

"Uh, yes. I'm here. Did you say *buy* a hospital?"

I nod, even though I know she can't see me. "Smithville Regional is no longer under contract with the association, so if you want a partner to open it as a not-for-profit entity, I'm interested. It will keep the hospital open, and it will have its own executive committee, not indebted to any large corporation."

Silence wafts through the phone, and I stare at Penny as we both wait for Andie's reply. If she doesn't go for it, I don't know what else to try.

"How?"

"Leave all the details to me. So... are you in?" I cross my fingers, and Penny does, too, but she also crosses her arms and eyes, making me laugh.

"On one condition."

"Anything."

"You have to tell Mitch in person."

Penny nods like a bobblehead, and I laugh. "Okay, but will you be there to catch me when I fall?"

"You better believe it."

I hang up with Andie and grab Penny in a hug. "I have to go."

"Where are you going?"

I glance back at my newly acquired office and without any regrets, I say, "I have to turn in my notice. I'm moving."

Penny's eyes grow wide with anticipation. "Will you take me with you?"

Aw. There is nothing more I would like than for her to move with me. Well, nothing more than having Mitch forgive me, but one thing at a time.

"What about cosplay? I doubt they have anything like that near Smithville."

Her eyes twinkle, and an evil grin spreads across her face. "You might be surprised about that."

We rush down the hallway to Matthew's office to drop the bomb-shell. He's going to be furious that I'm leaving, but more so that I'm taking his prized assistant with me. I love so much about my present job, but I really want a position that's more meaningful and, hopefully, less cut-throat. Plus, I'm hoping I can have a better work-life balance. Now, all I have to do is figure out a way to get Mitch to forgive me.

CHAPTER THIRTY-EIGHT
Mitch

News of the closing spreads like wildfire through the hospital. Before my shift wrapped up for the day, some people were already turning in their notices and looking elsewhere for employment, while others, like me, are determined to ride it out to the very end. It's the least I can do for the hospital that brought me into this world.

Regina taps on her phone in the ER break room, while I lean against the door after bringing in Fred Masters, who fell off a ladder while fixing his gutters. "How are you doing?"

I shrug. "Same as everyone else. I'm still mad as hell at her for letting us sink so she could rise."

She stares at me. "Stop jumping to conclusions. You don't know what she tried to do." Her words come out in a whisper. "You know for a fact she did something to ensure your license was intact. That says volumes. So if you're going to be all pissy, do it somewhere else."

"Wow. Someone's not getting any at home."

Steeling her eyes at me, she says, "More than you."

My eyes bug out of my sockets. *Ouch. Leave it to Regina to hit below the belt.*

"I'm sorry, Mitch. That was uncalled for."

Truth hurts.

Her face brightens as she focuses on something over my shoulder. I turn to see Clint standing there with a bouquet of roses. "You remembered." She rushes to him and wraps her arms around her neck.

"How could I not? You left huge hints the size of Texas every day this week." He cuts his eyes toward me. "It would have been our six-year anniversary today."

"Ah. So, are you going to start the clock over or just continue with this timetable when you get married again?"

Regina pops me on the shoulder. "Don't know and don't care."

She kisses him on the lips, and their embrace is both very touching and painful at the same time. I'm definitely going to be the bachelor uncle for eternity, but I must wear that title proudly.

He clamps a hand on my shoulder. "Have you heard from her?"

"Nope. Not even when I got the nerve to text her a thank you for not throwing me under the bus. She got what she wanted, and I guess I should be happy for her. She knows what she wants out of life and goes for it."

"I understand how big-city life can be overwhelming. After she got a taste of the good life down here, she could be rethinking her priorities. It happens."

"Pfft. I seriously doubt it."

He hands the flowers to Regina and gives her a kiss on the cheek. "I have to get to school before I get detention."

"Love you," she yells, followed by blowing him kisses.

Shoot me now.

While he rushes out the door, I glance at the ER desk. I've brought in a countless number of patients to this department. Most of them, I've known my entire life. I may be able to get a job in another city, but it won't be the same. The patients will be strangers. I won't know their medical histories already, like Stanley's A-fib or Mrs. Jackson's hypoglycemia.

I shake my head as I take a seat in the break room. Regina walks in and searches for a vase in the cabinet. "Aren't they pretty?"

"Lovely." Sarcasm drips from my reply.

"Stop being such a sourpuss."

"Stop being such a glass-half-full person. I'm tired of it, okay?"

Regina's jaw drops. "That's harsh. I'll have you know, other than Clint, you're my very best friend, not just a family member. I will always be here for you and always, always do my best every day to irritate the crap out of you."

I snort. "Ain't that the gospel?"

Jolene pops her head into the break room. "Regina, somebody's here to see you."

"Maybe it's your father, and he wants to know when you're going to get married... again."

She gives me the death stare. "Not funny," she says as she stomps out the door.

"What's her problem?" Jolene asks.

"Oh, I'm just aggravating her, as usual."

Jolene leans against the doorway and checks her phone. "I didn't get to thank you for taking care of Stanley last week. He's so cantankerous that I'm not sure if he would have come to the hospital had it not been for you being on duty that day."

I grin at her. She might be a busybody, but she does love her man. "Anything for Stan. He's a good guy."

"Yeah. I've been on him for years to lose weight, but he just loves Mrs. Cavanaugh's cooking too much."

"Don't we all."

She stares at the floor for a moment then asks, "Do you have any idea of what you'll do once the hospital closes?"

"I'm trying to take it one day at a time right now. You?"

"There's an opening at the home health company in Moultrie. I may try that. Better hours, less stress." She shrugs.

We stare off in silence for a while until we hear the radio at the nurses' station go off.

Jolene groans. "Sounds like another patient is coming in. I need to go."

Bit by bit, this place is being ripped apart, and there's nothing any-one can do about it. If one more person tells me, "It's not personal, it's business," I think I'll scream.

Regina rushes into the break room. "Hey, Mitch. I've got a patient I need help with. Do you mind?"

"Are *you* trying to get me in trouble this time? You know the last time I did a favor… didn't turn out so good."

She laughs. "I promise, you won't get in trouble. You really are the only person on the planet who can help me with this."

Before I can refuse, she leaves. "But…" I sigh and get up to follow her down the hallway toward bay number three.

On a dime, she swings around to me and shoves her phone in my hand. "You might want to see this." On her screen is a PowerPoint pre-sentation. As I scroll through the slides, I see pictures of myself, my niece, and several citizens of the community in Jackie's presentation. The last slide is Jackie's recommendation: to keep the hospital open.

Jackie did try to save the hospital after all. Even though she risked her career, she did attempt to do the right thing. I only wish it would have been enough. I stumble backward and bump up against the wall.

In the hallway, Regina flips open a chart and reads, "Now that we have that taken care of, let's focus on our patient. Female, age thirty, suf-fering from a broken heart. She tried this, but it didn't work." Regina holds out an EpiPen.

Regina kisses my cheek and flicks my nose. "Don't let her get away this time."

She shoves me into the exam room and scoots away. When I pull back the curtain to find Jackie sitting there in one of those not-so-sexy examination gowns, waving her fricking Smithville High School foam finger, my heart beats out of my chest while my lungs stop functioning.

CHAPTER THIRTY-NINE
Jackie

Mitch freezes when he sees me sitting on the exam table. His expression is unreadable. I'm not sure if he's happy to see me or if he's plotting my demise, but he looks delicious, even more so than I remembered. It's like I'm seeing him again for the first time. The rush of feelings comes back to me, and I want to wrap my arms around him. I'm afraid he'll push me away, so I sit tight in this breezy exam gown, my bare legs sticking to the paper barrier.

He clears his throat then glances around. "Are you lost?" His words come out all deep, croaky, and as sexy as sin.

"Yes."

Mitch points out the door with a shaky hand. "All you have to do is take the Ten Mile Road for about thirty miles, get on I-75 North for approximately five hours, and you'll be back with the other vultures."

I cock my head to the side. "Why is it called Ten Mile Road if it's thirty miles long?"

Mitch sneers. "Jackie, what are you doing here?" He snaps his fingers. "I get it. You're trying to catch me doing something out of my scope of practice again, right? This time, maybe you'll be promoted to president. How's that corner office, by the way?"

I stare down at my dangling feet and place the foam finger on the bedside table. "It's actually very lovely. On a clear day, I can see for miles."

He snorts. "I'm sure it suits you perfectly. If it's all the same to you, I have to get back into the ambulance. I still have a job to do—for a few more days, at least."

When he moves to leave, I say, "I quit my job."

Mitch halts in his tracks and only turns his head. "Why? No one to fetch you an Uber?"

I slide off the table, ripping the paper barrier on the gurney. I walk toward him, doing my best to keep my backside covered. Hospital gowns are quite drafty. "I'm so sorry."

"For what? For ruining so many lives, or for playing with my feelings? For wasting a hospital gown when you are clearly not hurt? I'll have to charge your insurance for that because I wouldn't want anyone to get special treatment. So, I'm going to ask you one more time. What exactly are you sorry for?"

Braving a touch, I reach out to wrap my fingers around his bicep, which tenses under my grasp. "I tried to keep the hospital open, but my boss vetoed my recommendation. I'm sorry for not telling you about the promotion and for pulling you into this whole mess. I'm sorry I let the entire community down. And I'm sorry for wasting a clean hospital gown. By the way, that was Regina's idea to make it look more authentic."

Mitch stares off and blows out a breath. "I appreciate your attempt, and on behalf of everyone in Smithville, you are forgiven. But why didn't you just tell me about the promotion from the start?"

"I don't have a valid reason for that, and I'm sorry. So very sorry."

"But why quit? You had everything you ever wanted."

"I had everything I *thought* I ever wanted. You changed me for the better. Or maybe you just brought out what was there all along."

He turns toward me, and my hand falls from his arm. "What was that?"

"I never really fit into the corporate world. It was all that I knew and what was expected of me. When I came here and realized there is so much more to life than the cut-throat world of ladder climbing. I love my job, but I want the perfect job and the perfect setting. I love

everything about this town: the pace, the people, especially *one* in particular."

His mouth twitches a bit, but no smile appears, so I continue.

"Whatever. It still doesn't make it right for you to call Mel. I told
you the truth. Were you hoping you'd find more evidence for your
case?"

Barely above a whisper, I say, "I called her because I was hoping she
didn't still hold a torch for you." I stare down at my feet and blow out
a breath. "That was not professional of me, but I wanted to make sure I
wasn't falling for someone who was taken."

I sneak a peek to see if my confession made a difference in his expression. He chews on his lip, and his eyes soften enough for me to feel
like I can continue.

"The moment I laid eyes on you, all the pieces to a puzzle I didn't
even know I wanted to complete fit together and made a perfect image—one that I could get used to for a very, very long time. You may
have saved me when I ate *your* pie..." I nudge him in the side. "But truth
be told, you saved me in every way possible. You shared your life, and
your family, with me, and I didn't realize how much I wanted that. I
need that."

Tears begin to fall, and I swipe them away. "And I don't think I ever
told you how much I really, really loved your pie."

He snorts.

My breath hitches. "And Chloe, sweet, precious Chloe. I want a
bunch of little Chloes in my life, but only if I can have them with *you*."

His eyes snap to mine, and for a moment, I think he's going to cut
and run. His chest rises and falls at a rapid pace. After what seems like
an eternity, he takes his thumbs and swipes the tears from my cheeks.
"You're not leaving?"

"Nope. In fact, Andie and I are partnering together to purchase the
hospital. By the first of the year, it should be a standalone, not-for-profit hospital, answering only to this community."

His eyebrows shoot up. "Are you serious?"

"As serious as an anaphylactic reaction. I now have a career that I'm thrilled about *and* the guy... if he'll have me."

He breathes so fast, I wonder if he's going to need emergency care. His big, strong hands cradle my face. Mitch smothers my lips, cheeks, and neck with kisses, and I never want him to stop. He comes up for air and asks, "Are you sure this is what you want?"

"Yes."

He picks me up and swings me around, my hospital gown flowing open, showing my butt cheeks, but I don't care. I haven't lost Mitch, and that's all that matters.

My body slides down his until my toes reach the floor again. "Are you sure you won't get bored here? You've pretty much seen all there is to this town. Not very exciting."

"Are you kidding me? There are chickens that roam the street. Then, there's the blog." I let out a breathy giggle. "Yes, I've read their entries, and they are quite thorough. Oh, and don't forget the festivals. I love food, so I'm kind of in love with this place. I'll just have to make sure I have my very own private EMT with me at all times. You know, just in case."

He kisses the tip of my nose. "As long as you know what you're getting yourself into." He gives me a playful nudge and adds, "Get dressed so we can take them off again in private."

That's what I'm talking about.

He watches as I throw my sweatshirt over my head and grins. "Mmm. Nothing sexier than a smart woman."

Heat rushes up my neck as I pick up my foam finger and stab him with it. "Watch it, buster."

"Oh, believe me, sweetheart. I am."

I shove him out the bay of the emergency room, and when we turn the corner to the ER station, a crowd erupts into cheers, making me jump backward. Andie and Gunnar, along with Regina and Clint, are there among some of the hospital staff, and they clap and "Woo-hoo" at us as we approach.

Andie gives me a big, bouncy hug. "I'm so glad you're staying. I promise, this is the best decision you'll ever make in your entire life."

She glances over at Gunnar, and he gives her a wink.

"Thank you for taking me in."

Andie holds out a fist to me. "To sisterhood." Regina runs over to add her fist to our pile, and I want to cry tears of joy this time. As much as I want to stay here and celebrate, by the expression on Mitch's face, he has other plans.

CHAPTER FORTY
Mitch

This past week has been a blur, and no one has been able to knock the smile off my face. Jackie and I have barely left the confines of my apartment over In a Jam, and it's been sheer paradise. I never thought I could be so happy, and all it took was a sweet, smart out-of-towner to charge in and upset my apple cart. My life will never be the same.

Wearing her corporate attire, she stands next to Andie and the director of the hospital to discuss the plans for the next phase of Smithville Regional Hospital. It's a scary undertaking, and it might not pan out, but with a lot of work and determination, it's definitely worth trying. And with the unanimous vote of approval from the new executive committee, it's starting off on a good note.

Regina stands next to me in the back of the room as Jackie unveils her plan, which is way above my pay grade to understand. We watch as she commands the room, and it's quite a sight to behold. When she puts her mind to something, nothing can stop her.

"She's a spitfire," Regina mumbles under her breath.

"You have no idea."

"Mitch, I'm so over-the-moon happy for you."

"Thanks. I guess things do turn out like they are supposed to, huh?"

Regina gives me a pointed "told ya' so" expression, making me chuckle.

I turn my attention back to Jackie, and when we lock eyes, her mouth turns up into a grin for just a second before she snaps back into business mode.

In my ear, Regina whispers, "Did I tell you that Clint is going to build us a house next to Gunnar and Andie? There is another plot of land on the other side. You know, in case you're interested." She waggles her eyebrows, and I grab her in a hug.

"We could have our own compound, like the Kennedys."

"Exactly."

While Andie discusses funding, Jackie's thumbs fly across her phone screen. Mine buzzes, so I glance down and see a text from her.

Jackie: *Are you bored yet?*

Me: *Not at all. You can be quite the bossy lady when you want to be.*

Jackie: *LOL. Wait till I get going.*

Me: *Is that a promise?*

I glance up to see her smiling at me. *Oh man, stick a fork in me. I'm done.* I have never felt this way about anyone. Jackie is perfect for me in every way possible, and we're only getting started good.

Andie holds up a finger. "Oh, I have one more item on my list. I want all EMTs to be certified as paramedics. Training will be paid for by the hospital."

Everyone in the room claps. My jaw drops, and I can't speak. Regina squeezes my arm as she jumps up and down. This day keeps getting better. She whispers, "That was my idea. I know how much you've wanted to advance."

I wrap an arm around Regina's shoulders and give my almost-sister-in-law a hug. A week ago, I would not have believed I could be this happy. No telling how I'm going to feel in a month or year from now.

As the crowd exits the room, chatting with excitement, I make a beeline toward Andie. "Thank you so much for everything."

Andie clutches her hands to her chest. "I should be thanking all of you. This community took me in when you all didn't have to. You gave me Smithville's finest as a fiancé. I *have* to give back. It's imperative."

"Hey now." Jackie slides up next to me. "You may have Smithville's finest, but I have the Smithville Stud."

Regina groans as my face turns beet red. "I'm out of here."

Jackie takes me by the hand and leads me to a corner of the room. "Well, what do you think?"

"I think you're incredible."

She rolls her eyes. "I mean, what do you think about the proposal?"

I slide a strand of hair behind her ear. "I think if you're in charge, it can't go wrong."

Jackie shakes a finger under my nose. "Just don't feed me another one of your pies, and we'll be good."

My head jerks back with laughter. "I'll figure out a new recipe."

She slides her hands around my neck. "I know you'll save me from whatever comes our way."

"This is loony. You know that, right, Elmer?"

"Completely nutty. Get it?"

"Ha-ha."

Then she kisses me, making my heart skip a beat. I know she's my lifeline, the one I've been waiting for. With her by my side, life will be so much sweeter.

I cup her face in my hands and say what I've wanted to say to her since the day I saved her life. I take a deep breath and say words I have never felt or said to anyone else. "Jackie, I love you so much."

She grabs me around the neck and squeezes me so tight, I think we'll both pass out. "I love you too. Are you ready to start this wild journey with me?"

"Yes, but I need to tell you something that may make you change your mind about all of this."

She scrunches up her brow, and I can feel the tension coursing through her body. "I'm listening."

With a straight face, I say, "No matter what happens, we will never, *ever* have chai tea here."

Jackie hip bumps me then takes me by the hand as we walk out of the conference room and down the hall to start our life together. It's going to be sweet, like pecan pie without the allergic reaction.

Acknowledgements

To Jamie, Jessica, and Kelly, for reading my words and being honest with me. My writing would suck so much more without you in my life.

To Jessica, Stefanie, and Erica (and all the Red Adept family), for believing in me.

To Molly Meeks, for your vast knowledge of cosplay.

To Mark, Maddie, and Jethro—you three make me smile every single day.

About the Author

After several decades of writing medical research documents, Cindy Dorminy decided to switch gears and become an author. She wanted to write stories where the chances of happy endings are 100% and the side effects include satisfied sighs, permanent smiles, and a chuckle or two.

Cindy was born in Texas and raised in Georgia. She enjoys gardening, reading, and bodybuilding. She can often be overheard quoting lines from her favorite movies. But her favorite pastime is spending time with Mark, her bass-playing husband, and Maddie Rose, the coolest girl on the planet. She also loves her fur child, Daisy Mae. She currently resides in Nashville, TN, where live music can be heard everywhere, even at the grocery store.

Read more at www.cindydwrites.com.

About the Publisher

Dear Reader,

We hope you enjoyed this book. Please consider leaving a review on your favorite book site.

Visit https://RedAdeptPublishing.com to see our entire catalogue.

Don't forget to subscribe to our monthly newsletter to be notified of future releases and special sales.

Made in the USA
Middletown, DE
30 April 2023

29750313R00136